Their lips met softly, questioningly. Tegan felt as though she'd waited all her life for this kiss. All that mattered was the velvet feel of Steve's mouth against hers, the strength in his arms as he held her. He was thoroughly male, and it fed her lonely soul….

As quickly as it had begun, it was over. Steve pulled away and looked deep into her eyes for what seemed like an eternity.

This is crazy, Steve thought. He had no business kissing her. What he should be concentrating on was how to steel his heart against the inevitable pain that was going to come when he proved the ranch belonged to him and he had to help her move out….

SUPER ROMANCE

Dear Reader,

For many years you have known and loved Silhouette author Robin Elliott. But did you know she is also popular romance writer Joan Elliott Pickart? Now she has chosen to write her Silhouette books using the Joan Elliott Pickart name, which is also her real name!

You'll be reading the same delightful stories you've grown to love from "Robin Elliott," only now, keep an eye out for Joan Elliott Pickart. Joan's first book using her real name is this month's *Man of the Month*. It's called *Angels and Elves,* and it's the first in her BABY BET series. What exactly is a "baby bet"? Well, you'll have to read to find out, but I assure you—it's a lot of fun!

November also marks the return to Silhouette Books of popular writer Kristin James, with her first Silhouette Desire title, *Once in a Blue Moon*. I'm thrilled that Kristin has chosen to be part of the Desire family, and I know her many fans can't wait to read this sexy love story.

Some other favorites are also in store for you this month: Jennifer Greene, Jackie Merritt and Lass Small. And a new writer is always a treat—new writers are the voices of tomorrow, after all! This month, Pamela Ingrahm makes her writing debut...and I hope we'll see many more books from this talented new author.

Until next month, happy reading!

Lucia Macro
Senior Editor

Please address questions and book requests to:
Silhouette Reader Service
U.S.: 3010 Walden Ave., P.O. Box 1325, Buffalo, NY 14269
Canadian: P.O. Box 609, Fort Erie, Ont. L2A 5X3

PAMELA
INGRAHM
COWBOY HOMECOMING

SILHOUETTE *Desire*®
Published by Silhouette Books
America's Publisher of Contemporary Romance

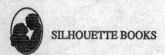

SILHOUETTE BOOKS

ISBN 0-373-05964-7

COWBOY HOMECOMING

Copyright © 1995 by Paula D'Etcheverry

PAMELA INGRAHM

is a native Texan, filled with true Texas pride. She lives in Austin, and is still madly in love with her high school sweetheart. She also says her two children are the greatest kids in the world. Her experiences in over fourteen years as a legal assistant provide just some of her story ideas, and being an accomplished seamstress and quilter take up her "spare" time. "Becoming a published author is a dream come true," Pamela says, and she plans to keep dreaming for a long, long time.

To my beloved husband, Bart—
the man of my dreams

One

Steve Williams felt the truck tires spinning, vainly trying for purchase on the mud-covered bridge. It wasn't helping matters that he had a fully loaded horse trailer straining the transmission. He felt more than saw the creek lapping threateningly over the wooden slats while the rain turned the unpaved road into a quagmire. Muttering under his breath, he backed up to make one more attempt. With Halloween just four days away, it looked like Mother Nature intended to give him a trick instead of a treat.

If he didn't get across now, he'd have to head back to Johnson City, and retreating was not in his nature. If he succeeded, he would be well and truly trapped. The only other way out was by horseback—through a hundred acres of uncleared scrub.

After reestablishing his mark, he carefully played the clutch to keep the tires grabbing for precious traction. He didn't release a tense breath, though, until the trailer was clear of the bridge and he was headed down the rutted lane to the old homestead. The windshield wipers made little headway against the sluicing torrent of rain, and his head-lights barely cut into the inky blackness. He crept along the track; his visibility was almost nonexistent and the condition of the road abysmal. This was worse than trying to land a Tomcat on a carrier in a hurricane. But he figured he'd get through this, too.

If Billy had let the road deteriorate, he could only imagine what shape the house would be in. His worry increased as he considered that Uncle Patrick would never have let this happen. Steve had always thought Billy was as honorable a man as his dad had been. He hoped his faith would not be proved misguided.

He supposed he should plan on keeping a fire going in the fireplace to ward off the bone-chilling cold of this norther. No doubt the propane tanks were dry, and with the rain turning to sleet soon, he wanted to be snuggled inside his sleeping bag when it hit. And maybe stay there until after Christmas.

Turning the heater up a notch, Steve smiled despite the rut that sent his head wrenching backward. It was impossible to drive this path without memories overwhelming him. Grandad and Gran had been dead for what—ten years now? They'd moved back from the city the minute he'd left for college. Grandad never had cottoned much to city dwelling. But if Billy hadn't kept up with his end of the bargain and let the place go to seed ... Well, it didn't matter. Steve knew he could whip the place into shape in no time.

The old house wasn't that big anyway. But size, he reminded himself, was irrelevant. He was looking for peace, solace. Solitude. Things not definable by length and width. It would suit him just fine if it rained for a month and the only things that could reach him were carrier pigeons.

Thunder rolled overhead in huge waves, vying for attention with the jagged lightning that rent the sky. The bursts of light cast the area into relief in strobelike vignettes, like the opening and closing aperture of a camera—all light, then darkness. A lot like the sky at night during a firefight. The thought made his neck twinge.

Nothing, except maybe being strafed by a MiG right now, could have surprised him more than seeing the glowing flicker of light in the kitchen window as he pulled to a stop in the yard. The rest of the house appeared as pitch dark as the night around him.

Squatters! He muttered a curse under his breath. If they thought they could commandeer Gran and Grandad's place like some flophouse, they had another think coming.

Reaching inside the glove compartment, he checked the clip in his 9 mm SIG-Sauer before he slipped it into his belt. He yanked his slicker around his shoulders before jamming his Stetson on his head. With an oversize flashlight that could double as a formidable baton in hand, he raced toward the back porch.

Taking a deep breath, he pushed the screen out of his way as he threw open the door. The incongruous thought hit him that he was glad he hadn't had to kick it in.

Time seemed suspended as he took in the scene at a glance.

She was beautiful.

No, she was stunning.

She sat at the table with an oil lamp off to one side. The wind whipped in and made the flame dance wildly. The lamp flickered and finally returned to a degree of steadiness, sending shadows over her face, and played with the highlights in her long hair. A section of the honey-colored tresses had swept forward over her shoulder and a curl lay against her breast like a child's hand. Her eyes were huge and he watched fear overtake her face.

She shivered.

Real time snapped into place as the screen door hit him in the back. "Who are you and what are you doing in my house?"

The woman shot to her feet, looking around for—he guessed—a weapon. A butcher knife lay in the drainer, and he could see her gauging her chances of getting it before he did.

"Don't even think about it, lady. Now, answer my question."

He admired the fact that she held her ground, throwing her shoulders back and meeting his eyes despite the fear in hers.

"My name is Tegan McReed. Who are you and what are you doing in *my* house?"

Steve noticed then that spread out across the table was a mountain of pictures, articles, and letters—about him. It was all the information he'd sent home to Grandad and Gran over the years, although any chronology would note that the letters and pictures had been fewer and farther between as time had gone on. He felt a familiar pang of regret.

After hanging his Stetson on the antique hat rack by the door, he pulled off the dripping slicker and tossed it into the corner. When his face was revealed, he watched as her eyes darted from him to the pictures on the table and back again. Clean-shaven, he looked younger than his thirty-three years. Which was only one of the reasons he planned to boycott razors for the next month.

"I'm Steve Williams. And this is my gran and grandad's homestead. Rather, mine now that they're gone."

Something blazed into her eyes, rivaling the lightning that split the night. "Like hell it is! I bought this property over two years ago. I have a marshal's deed to prove it."

Steve snorted derisively. "Lady, I don't care if you've got a dispensation from the Pope. I inherited this place years ago. And I sure as shootin' have never put it on the market."

"I bought it at auction. For nonpayment of taxes."

"My cousin has kept up the taxes on this place ever since I went into the service. He runs his cattle on the land."

"I'm afraid you're mistaken."

Steve rolled his eyes. "As stimulating as this game of 'no, I'm not,' 'yes, you are' is, it's not getting us very far. You've been duped, lady. I sure hope you haven't bought any bridges lately. The one in Brooklyn isn't for sale, either."

Tegan's eyes narrowed. "Forgive me if I'm not charmed by your wit, Mr. Williams. Now, I have every confidence that we can work this out through my attorney. I'll meet you at the offices of Koss and Koss in Johnson City tomorrow. So if you'd care to just leave—"

"I do not care to, lady! First of all, I barely forded the creek to get here. There's no chance of getting out until the water goes down. Second, tomorrow is Saturday and I don't know any attorneys who work on the weekend. So even if I wanted to—which I don't—I can't leave."

Fear spiked higher in her face. "You have to. You can't stay here."

"Lady—"

Something in her snapped. "You asked me for my name and I gave it to you. Use it!"

What had she said? Theresa? Tammy? No, something unusual. Tegan! That was it. "Tegan, I can and I will stay here. It's raining the mother of all storms out there. I'm going to be lucky as it is to find the barn still standing."

"That's it!" Her face brightened. "The barn isn't in the greatest shape, but it'll be all right for a while yet. You can bunk there until we work this out."

He looked at her as though she'd just grown a wart on her nose. "You must be out of your mind. I'm sure as blazes not bunking with my horse when I have a perfectly good house with a perfectly good fireplace where I plan to unroll my perfectly good sleeping bag. Or, if I'm lucky, my bed is still upstairs."

"It is, but that's not the point. This situation is simply not acceptable."

Steve ran a cold, weary hand over his face and back through his hair, futilely trying to wring out some water. "If you're not happy, you're welcome to leave. I need to tell you, though, it's going to be one heck of a long ride out the back of the property. But I'd be delighted to loan you my extra rain gear if you'd like. Now, if you'll excuse me, I'm going to get my things."

"No, I don't excuse you. You can't just barge in here and start giving me orders. This is my house, until it gets proved otherwise. And I haven't issued you an invitation to stay."

Once again Steve felt a surge of admiration, even as it paralleled a surge of annoyance. And he had to admit that he was the one who'd barged in on her, not the other way around.

He took a deep, calming breath and released it slowly. "Tegan, I apologize for being so brusque. I'm wet, I'm cold, and I'm tired. Add to that, I'm as confused as you are." He ran his fingers back through his hair again. "I don't mean to scare you, but if I wanted to hurt you, whether I stayed in the barn or not is irrelevant. I could always just break in during the night. There's no one to hear you scream, anyway."

If his intent had been to reassure her, he'd failed miserably. If she had to be honest, though, he'd simply voiced the thoughts running through her head.

It still made her mad.

"If I were you, I wouldn't bet that I'm helpless."

"I didn't say you were helpless, merely vulnerable. There's a difference."

"I'll consider myself warned."

"I wasn't warning you, either. I'm not a threat, Tegan." Her raised eyebrow challenged him.

"To your physical safety, then," he amended.

He held her eye for a long moment before he heaved another sigh. "All right. If it's that important to you, I'll bunk in the barn for tonight. But I won't stay there indefinitely."

Realizing how foolish her argument was, in light of his insight regarding the relative safety of having him in the barn versus the house, Tegan reconsidered. Besides, if he was in the house, at least she'd know where he was. If he stayed in the barn, she'd have no idea where he might be skulking about.

"No, you can stay in your old room. Just don't try anything funny."

Steve tossed his hands up. "I wish you'd make up your mind."

"I just did. But if you keep bickering with me, I can always change it again."

Tegan would have bet every dime she had that Steve's thoughts contained one exasperated word—"Women!" And from the look on his face, she was glad he bit back whatever else he might have been thinking afterward. Without a backward glance he retrieved his slicker and hat and shoved the screen out of his way. The frame banged with a certain finality as it rebounded against the side of the house.

Despite her change of heart, Tegan thought for a moment about rushing over and locking the door. Then she dismissed the idea just as quickly. The uncouth cowboy would probably kick it down and she was too proud of her handiwork to risk it unnecessarily. And even though it pained her, she had to admit the house wasn't very safe. The dead bolt wouldn't stand a chance against someone determined to break in.

Then sanity reminded her that she had precious seconds to arm herself. Grabbing a flashlight off the drainboard, she raced through the living room and up the stairs. She tore into her room, struggling to control her shaking hands as she lit the lamp on top of her dresser. Digging frantically, she found her .35 calibre snub-nose. It was small enough for her to handle but big enough to get anyone's—including a thick-headed cowboy's—attention. In fact, if the dunderhead thought she didn't know how to use it, it would be the worst mistake he ever made.

During the divorce, the Weasel had made the error of thinking she was going to roll over and take whatever he dished out—and had been proved wrong. There was no reason to give Cowboy the wrong idea from the start in this situation. She'd been cheated on and pushed around for the last time in her life. The Weasel hadn't gotten away with it and neither was Mr. Annapolis-Graduate-Turned-Cowboy.

She slipped the gun into the pocket of her drawstring pants, pulling the strings tighter to keep them up with the heavy weight, and bloused her sweater over the telltale bulge. Checking the mirror, she decided that with her hand in her pocket she managed a creditable job of looking casual and only a little suspicious.

As she started downstairs, she also decided she felt just the slightest bit foolish. Everything she'd been reading about Steve Williams made her think she should be looking closer for a halo instead of horns. And maybe a little of the foolish feeling came from the fact that she'd been mooning over his pictures a few short minutes ago. She'd been thinking how incredibly handsome he was in his Navy whites with his dark locks perfectly groomed and his deep brown eyes so serious. She winced, recalling that she'd sighed over the next picture that had shown him posing confidently, arrogantly, in his flight suit with his helmet tucked under his arm. This time his hair looked wind-kissed, and his grin had been devil-may-care, revealing beautiful white teeth.

Standing in her doorway, however, with the storm flashing behind him and his eyes blazing with anger, it was obvious Steve Williams might be a handsome man, but there was no doubt he could be a dangerous one. *Besides, everyone knows how wild those pilots are,* she thought as she decided she'd rather be safe than sorry. After all, there was no reason for Mr. Top Gun to know about her protection anyway, unless he tried something stupid.

By the time she'd returned downstairs and had put a kettle of water on the propane stove to heat, she had mostly convinced herself that a man who sent his grandmother long letters filled with affection—along with snapshots of himself taken everywhere from Paris to Honolulu—couldn't possibly be an ax murderer or a rapist. A little voice in the back of her head asked her what psychopaths usually looked like, but she hushed it.

She looked up when the cowboy came in from the deluge, dripping wet from brim to boots. He didn't so much as glance her way. He simply set down a cooler with a box stacked on it and headed back out. Three trips later, he carried two more boxes and what she guessed was a bedroll wrapped in green plastic. Then he took off the slicker, although it hadn't been of much use, and tossed it down in the corner as before.

Gritting her teeth, Tegan smiled archly. "You can put all your wet things in the laundry room. There's a gas furnace you can light to dry your stuff out."

She regretted her efforts at politeness when he cut her a glance and said, "I know where the furnaces are."

It looked for a moment as though he would ignore her hint about the laundry room, but after consideration he picked up the slicker and hat and took them into the utility area.

She glared at his retreating back. "And don't you dare walk on my hardwood floors in those boots!" she called. She hadn't spent two weeks on her hands and knees stripping and sanding years of neglect away, and then another week waxing and buffing, to let some clodhopper destroy it in one muddy trip upstairs.

Glancing at the table, she started clearing the mess she'd made. She paused as she picked up a picture, obviously an enlargement of a snapshot, but the sight of the six-foot-three or four-inch seaman with his arm draped around the shoulders of his maybe-five-foot grandmother made it difficult for Tegan to imagine him as a killer. Or psychopath of any type.

Then the little voice was back, and it reminded her that she was hardly an excellent judge of character. After all, she'd married the Weasel, hadn't she? People change. The Weasel certainly had. Or had he? Maybe he'd been the way he was from day one of their courtship through the last bitter day of their divorce. She just hadn't been paying attention. She gave herself some forgiveness because she'd been so young, but she was now far older and wiser than her mere thirty-one years.

She finished tidying, putting the letters and pictures back in the big envelope she'd found them in. It seemed wrong to be sorting through someone's private papers when the object of those memories stood in the flesh not more than twenty feet away. When he'd only been a photograph, she'd been intrigued, like she'd stumbled onto a mystery. Now she felt like a voyeur.

She was curious as to what he could be doing in the utility room, but the sound of thumps and grunts only created more questions than provided answers. She resisted the impulse to go in and check. Instead she fixed herself a cup of tea and headed back upstairs. All too soon he'd be out and they'd have to come to an agreement with regard to the sleeping arrangements.

She hoped she'd made it clear that his only option was his old room. She glanced around the master bedroom, and had to smile. It was a rather grandiose name for such a tiny space, but it had a saving grace—a picture window that revealed a breathtaking view of the rolling hills of central Texas.

The brass bed, which took up most of the space, was her favorite thing in the room. Amazed to find it in the house, she hadn't questioned the gift. Until now.

Opening the top drawer of the dresser, she took out a picture of a dashing soldier in his World War I uniform, smiling into the camera as he held his tiny German bride against his side. She wondered at the bravery of a man who would fall in love with the "enemy," defying convention to send his war bride home to live with his parents until he could come back. She touched the edge of a fragile, yellowed envelope. The love story she'd read in those letters had moved her to tears more than once. And with every word the house had come alive, no longer just wood and nails and rock and mortar, but a symbol of love and passion. She didn't think she could bear to give it up.

"He's just wrong," she said, lifting her chin. "That's all there is to it. I bought this place and all the contents."

A nagging doubt asked her if a heritage this rich had been stolen from her, how would she feel?

"Oh, shut up," she said, slamming the bureau shut.

"But I haven't said anything yet."

She whirled around to find Steve in her doorway. Her heart nearly stopped. He was still wearing his jeans but he had taken off his shirt and boots. She didn't think she'd ever seen anything sexier in her life than a wet cowboy in damp jeans that clung to every inch of him from his waist to his ankles. He had a big duffel bag slung over his shoulder, and the weight of it made the muscles in his arm bulge.

Her mouth went dry.

"I, uh, wasn't talking to you."

He cocked an eyebrow, and she could almost hear him hum the "Twilight Zone" theme.

"I'm not insane," she assured him. "I've just been alone for so long I don't realize that I talk out loud sometimes."

"Believe me, I understand."

She was surprised that the tone of his voice was not mocking. For some crazy reason, she did believe him. It might have been a combination of what she'd learned about him from his letters, or maybe it was just intuition, but she had the distinct feeling that Steve understood loneliness.

The moment became uncomfortable as they stood there, the thunder echoing dully down the hallway.

"Well," she said, clearing her throat. "Since we seem to be at a stalemate here, I guess we'll just have to make the best of it."

"I guess so."

"Your bed's still in there." She indicated the room two doors down with a toss of her head.

"That sounds rather like 'take it or leave it' to me."

Tegan pulled her shoulders back. "Something like that, yes."

He looked past her into the bedroom. "The bed looks beautiful. My grandad bought that for Gran for their anniversary one year. Gran nagged him on end that he'd spent too much money."

"I found the oddest mix-match of furniture I'd ever seen—everything from that Broyhill desk to a flea-market couch. The bed is the best example—the mattress and box spring were gone, but that beautiful brass frame was here."

"I let my cousin use this place as a hunting lodge, so I'm assuming that over the years stuff got hauled here as sort of a makeshift storage/lodge."

Steve stepped into the room and ran a finger over the top of the dresser. "My grandfather made this and the highboy."

Tegan was intrigued by the memories she sensed in his lost expression. But almost as if aware of her scrutiny, he snapped back his attention and became cold and inaccessible again.

"We have a lot to talk about, you know."

Her voice took a mocking tone. "No kidding."

"Not tonight, though. I'm going to hit the sack." He took a step down the hall and then turned back. "Oh, by the way. You won't need that." He nodded toward her hip. "Your virtue is safe with me."

Tegan's mouth fell open but Steve was gone. She looked down and saw that only the tip of the gun marred the line of her pants. Her sweatshirt fully concealed the rest. She could have had a hundred different things in her pocket. How had he known?

Despite his assurances, Tegan lodged a chair under the doorknob that night. It didn't help. She slept in fits and starts, waking at every odd sound. She may have gotten used to the creaks and groans the old house made, but she certainly wasn't used to a total stranger sleeping twenty feet away.

Morning couldn't come soon enough.

Two

Steve listened to the rain as it beat softly on the tin roof. It felt so comfortable, so right. The house Grandad had rented closer to town while Steve was in high school had never had this feeling. He'd always felt a bit guilty for the move anyway, but even as a teenager he'd understood that his grandparents were getting older, and it was a strain to haul him from the ranch to school for practices sometimes twice a day. Not to mention the football games themselves. He'd missed the ranch during those years. He and Grandad would come out on weekends to work, but that wasn't the same. He'd helped move Gran and Grandad back where they belonged right after graduation. That short summer before he'd left for college had reminded him that this, truly, was home.

Thunder rumbled faintly in the distance, just teasing the edges of his hearing. If he tried, he could almost pretend he was eight again, or maybe ten, and the rain would be falling and he'd catch muffled traces of Gran's and Grandad's voices down the hall. He'd hear Grandad's deep baritone and then Gran's sweet contralto as she answered in her gentle laugh.

Only the woman in the bed down the hall wasn't Gran. She was an intruder in his house, and he perversely refused to let her infringe on his memories, as well. Just as he refused to think about what she looked like stretched out across that brass bed, her long hair fanned on the pillows—

With a growl, he swung his legs out of the bed and sat up as he reached for the flashlight he'd placed on the nightstand. He thought about lighting the lamp but decided the soft glow of lantern light would make the setting much too romantic. He figured he needed to set a precedent from the very beginning that no matter how beautiful Tegan McReed was, no matter how soothing the sound of rain on a tin roof, no matter how quaint the setting—he was not going to act like a soft-hearted fool.

He grabbed his pants and pulled them on with a jerk. If he couldn't sleep, he might as well tend to his horse and get his things organized.

He opened the door slowly and stepped down the hall in his socks, his shoes tucked under one arm. He paused by Tegan's door and in the echoing silence of the house he heard the rustling sound of limbs against sheets. She sounded restless. He found it hard to be sympathetic when his night had been much the same. Heading for the stairs, he avoided the fourth step and its telltale squeak at the last second and, despite his current ill humor, he smiled. Some habits were everlasting.

The sweet smell of furniture polish assailed him in the darkness and a swell of memories hit him in a wave. In the darkness he could just as easily be twenty years in the past, sneaking out of the house to meet his buddies.

Stepping to the fireplace, Steve stared at the bed of dying embers. Finally, with a resigned sigh, he set the flashlight on the mantel and braced his hands against the cool wood.

He closed his eyes.

Christmas. First rifles for Billy and him. Freezing in the deer blind. Getting that first buck. Racing into the bushes to throw up.

He shook his head and the memories shifted.

High school. Football games. The pride of the fighting Jaguars. Throwing pass after pass. Billy never missing a catch. The Killer Cousins. An unbeatable team.

Prom. Anita Sue Andrews. The back seat of the old Plymouth.

The bash before he left for Annapolis. Half the town eating barbecue.

And always, Gran and Grandad. Side by side. Proud. Sad.

Steve twisted his head around. He sensed her before he heard her. He stood perfectly still in the inky darkness, smiling when she paused and carefully avoided the fourth step.

She moved with an unconscious grace despite her obvious grogginess. His groin tightened as the soft lamplight revealed a half-lidded, sleepy expression that was sexy as hell.

He waited until she was almost at the kitchen before he said softly, ''Mornin'.''

Tegan gasped as she whirled around. Her heart was in her throat as she raised the lamp. It cast a circle of light in front of her, hardly reaching him. She squinted, knowing who it was but needing to see him.

''You startled me,'' she said, hating the breathless catch in her voice.

He didn't speak, didn't move from his place in front of the fireplace. No apology for scaring her witless.

What was she expecting?

She supposed she should thank him. She'd been stumbling down the stairs still half asleep. If nothing else, she was fully awake now.

She turned up the wick and the room brightened a bit more. It felt awkward to simply stand there, and it would have been rude to just turn and walk away. The darkness, however, felt too close, too intimate, so she filled the silence by lighting two more of the oil lamps she'd placed around the room. By the time she was done, the biggest of the shadows had been dispelled.

And still he watched. Not moving. Silent.

It made her edgy.

"The room's pretty."

"Thank you," she said, even though she wasn't sure his grudging comment was actually a compliment.

The dark wood of the couch supported deep green cushions. Accent chairs flanked each side, upholstered in burnished gold. Throw pillows added bright swirls of color, and the polished coffee table caught the glow of the lamps and cast the light back.

She glanced at him after she fluffed a pillow and saw his attention riveted on the Mariner's Compass she'd made the focal point of the far wall.

"Did you do that?" he asked with a nod toward the quilt.

She nodded.

"My gran was a quilter."

Tegan wasn't sure what to say. "It's a fascinating art."

Her heart swelled with pride as she looked at her masterpiece. Before she was through, she intended to hang her quilts on every appropriate piece of wall in the house as a constant and pleasant reminder that she was talented and creative and imaginative—all the things the Weasel had tried to make her believe she wasn't.

Shaking away the thoughts of her ex, she looked back at Steve. He seemed lost in his thoughts. She saw his gaze stray to the wooden rocker she loved to sit in while she quilted, and wondered if he pictured his grandmother there.

She thought about the trunk she'd found in the attic. She started to speak, but realized she wasn't ready to reveal that yet. Instead she asked, "Do you have any of her quilts?"

"Just two. I was too foolish to realize their value until I was older."

Tegan watched, amazed, as he straightened his shoulders and walked away into the kitchen. And here she'd been concerned about being rude! Obviously she needed to quit worrying.

Feeling like a puppy at heel, she followed. By the time she entered the kitchen, he had already lit the lamp on the counter. She pulled out the coffeepot and started filling it.

"Would you like some coffee?" she asked over the sound of the water.

"Yes," he said as he moved into the utility room.

"You're welcome," she muttered to herself as she counted scoops of fragrant grounds into the filter.

She heard him rummaging around and tried not to be curious. Instead, she waited impatiently for the coffee to finish and turned off the stove. Determined not to wait on him, she fixed herself a large mug, covered it, and shrugged into her coat and slicker. Steve rounded the corner from the utility room just then and gave her a once-over. Tegan felt her lips tightening.

"Coffee's ready," she said tersely. "I'm going to the barn."

"Wait a minute and I'll go with you." He executed an about-face and went to retrieve his slicker.

Tegan's hands clenched into fists. There was no doubt in her mind that he had just given her an order. And she'd have a lobotomy before she'd stand around and obey a total stranger who'd barged into her world and was trying to take over.

Grabbing her coffee and a flashlight, she headed out of the house.

Steve heard the door slam and rolled his eyes. He was just trying to be gentlemanly, for heaven's sake.

As he stood in the kitchen with his gear, the bulb overhead flickered and came on. The soft lighting changed to harsh fluorescent and revealed details he'd missed the night before.

Tegan had obviously spent a lot of time on the place. The cabinets had been painted a sunny yellow and the trim was forest green. The knobs had delicate, hand-painted flowers on their porcelain faces. She'd chosen white pine for the furniture and the curtains were snowy white and frilly. Steve had the obscure notion that the room suited Tegan perfectly—which was an insane musing to have about the woman who was squatting on his property!

Blowing out the lamp, he put it down on the counter by the telephone. He picked up the receiver and tried to call his cousin, but wasn't surprised when he got a recording that said his call could not be completed as dialed. He'd keep trying to reach Billy through the day until the lines got cleared up.

As he looked outside, he flipped the switch for the flood lamps. The beams cut a path into the drizzly, dark morning, but as he sloshed across the yard, he guessed that by the time he finished in the barn, the sun should be up enough for him to take Ghost Dancer on a ride.

The interior of the barn was warm and welcoming. Ghost Dancer whinnied when the door opened, and Tegan's horse stuck her nose over the edge of her stall, as well. A mouser of indeterminate heritage jumped down from the workbench and wound itself around his legs, its purr loud in the quiet surroundings.

Steve crouched to give the insistent feline a friendly rub before stopping to stroke the mare's beautiful muzzle. Her large brown eyes were friendly and curious.

"Good morning, girl. Hungry?" She delicately lipped the apple out of his hand, not offering an answer to his next question of, "Where's the boss?"

Ghost Dancer accepted Steve's firm pat on his neck as though it were his due and grabbed at his snack.

"Greedy mule," Steve scolded affectionately, adding one last pat before he fed both of the horses. While they crunched contentedly, he went to work separating his gear. He had already draped his saddle over a railing, but he needed to sort his bridles and halters from his duffel bag. When he was finally ready, he saddled Ghost Dancer and led him out into the yard.

Once mounted, Ghost Dancer tossed his head, eager for a bit of exercise, but Steve kept him in check. His own heart wished desperately for an all-out race with the wind, to experience even the simulation of flying, but the ground was slippery and would be treacherous in places. Instead, both he and Ghost Dancer would have to settle for a long, sedate ride.

At the slow pace he set, the trip to the creek took almost fifteen minutes. Although close, it still hadn't crested its banks. It was comforting to remember that the water usually went as quickly as it came. If the rain would let up, it would be passable in a day. Two at the most.

Steve let out a dry laugh at his next thought. His latest ex-girlfriend, who loved to dabble in armchair psychology, would probably offer some analogy comparing his anxiety about crossing the creek to a deep-seated fear of change or risk. Which would be a stupid thing to say to a fighter pilot.

His shoulders dropped a little.

Ex-fighter pilot, he reminded himself.

Shaking off his melancholy, he turned Ghost Dancer to walk with the stream. He didn't know what had brought Maryanne to mind. She hadn't even been very good at her analyses, except for what she'd said just before she'd said goodbye. "There's no room in your life for anything that doesn't have wings."

She'd nailed it. Being an aviator was his life. And he'd been a damn good one, too. After the injury, he'd been so lost even the offer to fly refuelers hadn't lured him. Even though the refuelers were unsung heroes, it wasn't for him. He also found that the intrigue of the Naval Intelligence Service wasn't enough to fill the void.

He'd finally given in to the Navy shrink and agreed to take some time off. With nothing to keep him in New Orleans, he'd headed to the closest thing he'd ever had to a home. To be honest, he just wasn't in the mood to deal with this situation right now. In a way he felt sorry for Tegan, but he wanted her off his property, and the sooner the better.

The image of her face when he'd burst through the door came to mind in vivid detail. Not surprisingly, there'd been fear, and he regretted that now. But regardless of the circumstances, she was still in for a painful lesson about being too trusting. Someone had bamboozled her, but there was no way he was going to let pity deprive him of his inheritance.

Tegan waited until Steve was out of the barn before getting off the bale of hay. She'd come in and headed straight for the loft to check for any more leaks in the roof. Grabbing the hooks, she'd hauled a bale over to fill the crib but had stopped when she heard him rummaging around below. With every sound he made, she struggled with her thoughts.

Kicking at a few loose straws of hay, Tegan fought off a wave of panic. Of course it would be all right. She'd done everything by the book. When she'd filed her deed, the clerk hadn't had to warn her that the previous owner had two years to challenge a sale based on delinquent taxes. She'd done enough title work to be well aware that she needed to wait before she made improvements to the property, but as time had gone on, she'd become more and more confident that everything was going to work out. She'd made only the most basic repairs to the house and even though the barn was desperately in need of attention, she'd held up investing any extra money, just to be safe.

Well, the two years had been up almost a month ago. She remembered the date quite clearly because she'd had her close friends Angelica and Enrique out for a celebratory dinner. Enrique had promised to help her reroof the barn when the weather permitted. They'd laughed and toasted the day with cider in front of a roaring fire.

It was just too bad that Steve had delayed filing an appeal. Another wave of fear rolled through her stomach, reminding her that she'd learned enough about the judicial system during her divorce to know what a lot of money and a clever lawyer could do. If the two-year limit had been up months ago, it might be one thing. But a few weeks? It scared her.

No! She forced the thought away, determined to be positive. He'd missed his deadline and that was that. She owned this place—lock, stock and broken-down barn. It was hers, by God, and she wasn't giving it up.

She finished filling the hay crib and climbed down from the loft. Steve had obviously fed Dream Chaser before he'd left and for a moment resentment swelled. Then she forced herself to relax as she turned Dream Chaser loose in the paddock.

An insistent meow at her ankle made her smile. "Hello, Good For Nothing. I can see that once again you've forgone your natural instincts and are waiting on me to feed you." The cat purred and butted against her hand for another rub. She set him on the workbench before pouring a packet of cat food into a bowl. "Just remember, if I find a mouse in here, you're history."

Good For Nothing had heard the threat before, but didn't believe it. He moved to attack his breakfast.

With the animals content, she mucked out the stalls and spread fresh hay. It was her least favorite chore, but an unavoidable one. She would tell Steve that she didn't want him doing her any favors. She'd take care of her own horse, and he could take care of his.

Wincing at the sullen thought, Tegan restalled Dream Chaser and brushed the horse down. She tried her best to put herself in Steve's shoes. She could only imagine how she'd feel to come home and find someone in her house claiming to own it. Despite the pity she felt, she hardened her heart and resolved that it wasn't her fault Steve had been careless. She hadn't set out to hurt him, but the fact remained that this was now her home. She loved it, and it was an important part of her life.

With her tasks finished, Tegan dusted her hands as she headed for the kitchen. She was welcomed by the smell of hot, fresh coffee. She poured herself a second cup and was busy stirring in cream when Steve came in, the screen banging shut behind him. She glanced over her shoulder as he closed the door, and her light, airy kitchen suddenly felt claustrophobic.

Not that it mattered, but he seemed even more handsome than he had last night. Despite his cowboy garb, he should have had a stamp on his forehead that said Military. His short black hair and inscrutable brown eyes went perfectly with his square, stubborn jaw. His dark chambray Western shirt fit across his shoulders as if it had been tailored for him, and she had the churlish thought that he seemed to have a bungee cord hooked between his shoulder blades to ensure his posture never slouched.

Her eyes were drawn down to where his shirt had been pressed against a taut, flat stomach and tucked into the waistband of faded jeans—jeans that fit snugly around his lean hips and lovingly caressed his thighs.

When she realized what she was doing, she jerked her head back around and concentrated on her mug.

"Thank you for cleaning Ghost Dancer's stall."

She nodded. "Thank you for feeding Dream Chaser."

He nodded, as well. "Did you exercise her?"

Tegan bristled. "I rode her yesterday before the storm hit. I don't need you to tell me how to take care of my horse."

Steve took a deep breath and let it out slowly. "I'm sorry."

Tegan let the tension drain from her shoulders. "Accepted. Does this mean we're going to talk now?"

"I reckon we've got to sometime, don't we?"

"Seems unavoidable."

"Did you know that barn is about to fall down?"

"Do you think I'm stupid?"

Steve rubbed his eyes. "This is about as productive as our conversation last night. Would you stop being so defensive?"

"I would be if your questions weren't so intrusive."

His smile was sardonic. "You'll have to forgive me if I'm not at my most charming. I'm a little confused."

"Join the club! I told myself I couldn't be timid if I moved out here, but I never expected a man to kick open my door in the middle of the night when I said it."

Still tight-lipped, Steve fixed himself another cup of coffee. Needing to move, she went to the refrigerator and started filling her arms with items for an omelet.

"Didn't everything spoil with the electricity out?" Steve asked in a dubious tone as he eyed her supplies.

"It's propane powered. I spent a small fortune on it since they don't make these babies in the U.S. anymore." She stroked the stainless-steel door when she went back for a tomato.

"A wise decision."

"We'll see if time proves me wise or not. So far, the electricity has only gone out twice for any bothersome length of time. The Pedernales Electric Co-op is pretty darn reliable."

"I know. I grew up here."

So much for mundane conversation. Tegan peeled and rinsed an onion, dicing methodically to conceal her renewed tension. "I'm going to fix an omelet. Would you care for some?"

She picked up a can of biscuits questioningly and waited for his, "Yes, thank you," before adding an extra portion to the cookie sheet.

"By the way, since you're cooking, I'll clean up."

"You won't get an argument from me," Tegan said, using her shoulder to wipe a tear away as she finished the onions and began to work on the tomato and cheese.

Almost absently, Steve added, "Gran never got too worried about blackouts. If anything thawed, we'd just have a feast."

"Since I don't have a family to feed, I don't have that option. I learned my lesson the hard way when I had to give away a half side of beef that had thawed. That's when I bought a portable generator to keep the freezer going."

She put the beaten eggs into the pan and added the trimmings. Bending over, she watched the burner as she turned the flame down and then moved to put the biscuits in the oven to brown.

"My grandad did the same thing—getting a generator, I mean. Billy must have it . . ." His voice trailed off and Tegan could almost feel him debating with himself about what to bring up next.

She was no detective, but she could guess that Billy was the cousin he'd spoken of yesterday who was responsible for the place. She wasn't about to ask for confirmation, though.

With her thoughts distracted, she grabbed the handle of the skillet without a pot holder. Yelping in pain, she hurried to the sink and turned on the cold water, thrusting her injured palm into the stream.

"Are you all right?" Steve moved quickly to her side. He looked uncomfortable and helpless. Oddly, the image helped calm her. He wasn't a heartless beast any more than she was a heartless thief. This would all work out somehow.

"Tegan, why don't we cut a deal? Let's get through breakfast, get to know each other a little bit, then we'll hash this out. Maybe that way we can avoid any more injuries." He gave her a boyish grin that immediately tugged at her heart. "And maybe a case of indigestion."

Her lips quirked. "I don't know if that's possible, but I'll take your offer." She left her wounded hand in the cold water and directed with the other. "The plates are up there, silverware here. Salsa's in the fridge."

Steve took over setting the table and rescued the biscuits before they burned. In moments they were settled across the table from each other.

"How's the hand?" Steve asked as she picked up her milk.

"Fine. Nothing serious."

"Good. I'm sorry I distracted you."

She shook her head. "Don't worry about it." She fiddled with her food, staring at the melted cheese and fluffy eggs before looking up to meet his dark eyes. A smile played at the corner of her lips. "I have an unfair advantage over you, you know. I already know a lot about you."

Steve tilted his head slightly. "I thought I recognized that pile of pictures on the table last night."

"I found them in the attic. I didn't mean to pry."

"How could you have been prying? Prying is a deliberate intrusion. You were just exploring."

Her face cleared. "Thanks, that makes me feel better."

"So—" he took a sip of coffee "—what did you learn?"

"That you're a Navy pilot, that your grandparents raised you, and that they loved you very much."

"It's naval aviator, but you've got the rest about right. You divined all that from a pile of pictures?"

"And from a scrapbook that was lovingly put together with every article ever written about you in the local paper and in the *Stars and Stripes,* and by the fact that every picture has been labeled with dates and events."

Steve's features turned sad. "Gran was unbelievable."

Tegan squirmed in her chair. "I'm embarrassed to admit that I read your letters to them. I—"

"Tegan, you could just as easily have burned them when you hauled trash. Don't apologize."

"I know, but now that you're here, I feel like a voyeur."

"I don't think I ever sent any of those kinds of pictures."

He delivered the line so completely deadpan, it took her a second to recognize his humor. She chuckled in surprise.

"Um, yes. So, are you still in the Navy? Being a pilot—um, aviator—must be exciting."

A look of deep pain flashed across his eyes before he masked his expression. "I'm 'active duty,' but I can't fly jets any more."

"What happened?" she asked before she realized how impolite the question was.

"I was injured in a skirmish over in the Middle East. I can't take the high G's now, so no aerial maneuvers for me."

"Steve, I'm sorry."

His shrug was nonchalant but Tegan instinctively knew better. His expression might be enigmatic, but inside, this man was angry and hurt.

"I'm working with Naval Intelligence now." He drained his coffee and set the cup on the table.

To twist a phrase from the army, it was a job, but it wasn't an adventure—at least, it wasn't the adventure he wanted.

"Now it's your turn, Tegan. Tell me about yourself. What are you doing alone out here in the middle of nowhere?"

"I wouldn't call this nowhere. Johnson City is only thirty minutes away."

He just looked at her.

"The truth is, I'm a professional quilter. I teach seminars, write books, and I'm thinking about opening a shop."

"Sounds..." He looked chagrined while he struggled for an adjective. "Interesting."

"It is. It's also a solitary career. But it suits me."

"If your Mariner's Compass on the wall in the living room is any evidence, you're terrific at it. I'd give anything if I knew where all the quilts Gran made were."

A pleasant warmth stole through Tegan as she decided to reveal her secret. "I found nine of them in the attic and right now they're with a friend who is a professional restorer. They'd been stuffed into a chest and, unfortunately, some of them have acid stains from the wood. Two had bad mold spots, but I think they're all going to come out fine. One of my favorites is her variation on the Drunkard's Path."

Her heart did a flip-flop at the way Steve's face brightened. He looked like a little boy who'd just been told he was getting a new bike for his birthday.

"That's great! I was afraid they were lost forever. Gran made a whole lot more than nine quilts, but I'm not going to look a gift horse in the mouth. Maybe Billy has the rest of them."

There was that name again. Tegan hardly claimed to be clairvoyant but she knew that Cousin Billy was going to mean trouble before this was all over.

When they both pushed back their plates, Tegan took a deep breath and said, "I plan on keeping you to your promise to clean up, but why don't we save the dishes for later? We'll adjourn to the living room. It's time to get this over with."

Steve followed her almost reluctantly. He couldn't help but notice the way her long, honey-colored hair rippled down her back, nor could he ignore the sensual sway of her hips as she led the way. He also remembered the fear he'd seen in her azure blue eyes as she'd steeled herself against this moment. In a matter of hours his conviction about teaching this woman a lesson had been replaced with a deep concern. But Tegan was right. It was time to get it over with.

She moved to sit in one of the armchairs flanking the couch. He sat on the end of the sofa closest to her and rested his elbows on his knees. He saw that she'd placed a file on the coffee table, and felt his gut clench.

"Steve, I don't know your side of the story yet, but believe me, I had no idea who the Williamses were who hadn't bothered to pay their taxes. You were just a name."

He nodded and indicated she should continue. Opening the file, she handed him a marshal's deed. "Just over two years ago, I bought this property at a foreclosure sale. I have a friend who works in the Blanco County tax office and she knew I was looking for a place small enough to handle but big enough to give me some room. We started watching this place almost four years ago, when the taxes first became delinquent. She told me about the place, but not to get my hopes up. When the taxes remained unpaid, I sent a letter to the county making an offer on it. After the taxes were a full two years delinquent, they accepted. I bought it and then waited almost another two years before I moved out here."

She took the deed back and closed her file. "I'm sorry, Steve. I don't know why you didn't keep up with the taxes, but I've waited four years to make a dream come true. This place is mine now."

Steve schooled his expression to reveal nothing of the riotous emotions going through him. The deed certainly looked authentic, but there were still a lot of questions he needed answers to. The problem was, the tiny voice in the back of his head that had been warning him to stay on top of Billy was now screaming at him. In the past four years he'd had two, maybe three, conversations with Billy. The buildup to the trouble in the Gulf, his injury, his recuperation, and the career change to the NIS, had kept him too busy to worry about the ranch. In one of his calls, Billy had mentioned that the depressed cattle prices were really starting to hurt, but Steve had never questioned him when Billy had said that everything was fine.

"After my grandfather got frail," Steve began, feeling he owed her some explanation, "my uncle was given permission to use our acreage to run his cattle, and all he was required to do was keep up the taxes. When my uncle died, I cut the same deal with his son, my cousin Billy."

Steve stood and started pacing. "Because of my injury and recuperation, I've let time slip away, and I haven't checked in with my cousin for—obviously—much too long. All I can tell you is, ranching meant everything to Billy. I know there's a mistake." He reached up to straighten a figurine on the mantel.

"Steve—"

"I'm telling you there's been a mistake!" he stormed as he jerked away from the fireplace. "The money's been credited to a wrong account or something. I'm sure the county will have to compensate you for your trouble, so don't worry about that.''

Tegan didn't respond, since there was no point in arguing. The thought that he could be right—that the county had made an error—scared her more than she could admit. She unconsciously burrowed back against the cushions, realizing that the day had barely begun. Tomorrow was Sunday, and even if the creek miraculously receded tonight, the courthouse was still closed.

Monday seemed an eternity away.

Three

***

Steve closed his eyes and took a deep breath. When he looked at her, his thoughts were filled with a mixture of thinking how beautiful she was—framed by the dark gold cushions and backlit by the track lights attached to the ceiling—and how much he wished he'd never laid eyes on her. He also noticed how she'd pulled farther back into the cushions, and felt her fear.

"Tegan, I apologize. You must be as uncomfortable as I am. Since there's nothing we can do until Monday, what do you say we start over? Let's set some ground rules until we can settle this."

Slowly, Tegan nodded. "All right. I don't know what choice we have except to pace around each other like caged lions, and I've vowed I'll never pace again."

After taking a deep breath, she flipped back the length of hair that had fallen over her shoulder. "But before we go any further, I'm going to light a fire. It always makes me feel better."

He looked at her oddly. "I can do that."

Her laugh mocked him. "What? Start a fire or make me feel better?"

Steve wondered what she'd do if he told her exactly what images her teasing remark had evoked. He was confident he could build a fire between them that had nothing to do with wood and matches.

His provocative smile caused her to blush.

"Look, Steve," she cut in just as he started to answer, "I'm sure you can get a fire going like every other Boy Scout, but I'm not asking you to. I've become quite good at it."

His body reacted to her innocent double entendre. For an instant he imagined her lying on the braided rug at his feet, her hair fanned out and spilling over onto the polished wood of the floor, the lights from the flames dancing over her skin—

Steve blinked to break his momentary lapse of concentration. What had she just said? When he remembered, a sour look crossed his face. "We're not going to spend the next two days playing 'anything you can do, I can do better' are we?"

Tegan seemed honestly surprised. "Of course not. I just meant—"

"Look, I'm going to make a confession. I'm still old-fashioned enough to open doors for ladies, pick up the tab at restaurants, haul packages from the car, and perform assorted other atrocities that now seem to be grounds for execution. So believe me when I tell you I'm not going to let you haul wood when I'm perfectly capable of being in charge of the fireplace for a couple of days. It's not that I don't think you can do it—just humor me, okay?"

She shook her head slowly from side to side but he could see amusement threatening to overwhelm the stern expression in her gorgeous blue eyes.

"If I let you do that, and I get found out, I'll have to forfeit my membership in the ISWF."

A grin twitched at his lips. "All right, I'll bite. What's the ISWF?"

"The International Society of Women Firebuilders. We have a very strict code of ethics, you see."

"And I suppose letting a man build a fire for you is a severe infraction."

"The worst."

"I'm afraid you're in a lot of trouble, then, because I'm about to do it."

Tegan managed a creditable imitation of a distressed Southern belle as she clutched a fist to her breast. "Oh, but, sir, you couldn't be so cruel."

Steve joined fully into the silliness. "Yes, my pretty," he said, rubbing his hands together with villainous glee and advancing to loom over her. "And I'm going to make you watch."

Tegan swooned against the chair. "Oh, what shall I do, what shall I do?"

Steve returned to the fireplace and started stacking logs. "How about making some hot chocolate?" he asked in a casual, normal voice.

Tegan sat up, giving him a mock frown. "Do you plan to do anything this weekend besides eat?"

Tilting his head, Steve gave her figure a serious once-over and quirked an eyebrow. "That's not eating, that's drinking. Besides, it'll keep my hands occupied."

Her flush deepened as she stood. "Well, just remember—you agreed to do the dishes if I cook."

"Deal. Oh, by the way, I like lots of marshmallows."

"So? Folks in the desert like water. Doesn't mean they get it."

"You're a hard woman, Tegan."

As she moved past him, she nodded arrogantly. "And don't you forget it."

He caught her arm, making her pause and look down at him. All teasing was gone when he simply said, "Thanks."

Shrugging one shoulder, she said, "No problem. We both needed to lighten up."

Her arm tingled where his hand had been as she went into the kitchen and began warming the milk. A quick search through the cabinet produced the cocoa, sugar, and finally a triumphant smile as she found the marshmallows.

When she realized she was actually trying to whistle, Tegan clutched at the spoon she was using to stir the chocolate concoction. It was one thing to be polite and make the best of the weekend, it was another thing entirely to be standing over a steaming saucepan of cocoa daydreaming about a broad set of shoulders and a great rear end bent over her fireplace. *Her* fireplace, she repeated firmly. If she didn't get her head together and stay aware that those gorgeous buns were after her property, she could lose her home before she even knew what hit her.

She reviewed her encounters with Steve so far and was bemused. Nothing was going as it ought to. They were enemies, weren't they? Yet moments before they had been bantering like friends. Her problem was, she liked things neat and orderly, for the rules to be defined and honored. Unfortunately, Hoyle hadn't written an instruction book for this situation. She was going to have to play it by ear.

Well, she might not have full control of the situation, but she was sure of one thing: she had to steel her heart to make things work out her way. Now was not the time to be getting soft. Steve seemed a likable enough guy, but she needed to remember that if he wasn't necessarily her enemy, he was certainly her adversary. It was one thing to be polite, and quite another to let her guard down.

With her pulse and her errant thoughts under control, Tegan turned off the stove and filled two oversize mugs almost to the rim. A thought suddenly occurred to her, and a quick trip to the freezer had a package of pork chops thawing in the sink. She returned to the cocoa and plunked several marshmallows in each cup. She carefully carried the treats back into the living room.

Steve had done a marvelous job on the fire and now lounged on the couch with his legs stretched out on the coffee table while he watched the flames intently. He sat up straighter to take her offering, smiling when he saw the fluffy white lumps floating on top.

"I knew you were bluffing."

"Oh, yeah? How?" Tegan asked as she maneuvered herself back into the chair without spilling.

"I had you pegged as a marshmallow kind of person."

Tegan's forehead furrowed. "I'm not sure how to take that."

He cut her a glance that contained a generous dose of teasing. "Any woman who names her horse Dream Chaser, makes quilts for a living, and paints little flowers on the cabinet knobs is a marshmallow kind of woman. Trust me."

She rolled her eyes. "This from a guy who named his horse Ghost Dancer and sent his grandmother snapshots of himself in a hula skirt and lei."

Steve raised his chin to look down his nose at her. "That is entirely different."

Tegan smirked. "Uh-huh."

They sipped in silence except for the friendly crackling and popping from the fireplace. Just as she was beginning to relax for what felt like the first time that day, Steve drained his cup and stood.

"I'm going for a refill and to try my cousin again. You want anything?"

She declined and watched him as he retreated to the kitchen. It was all she could do not to edge closer to the door and eavesdrop on his conversation. Curiosity warred with integrity, but integrity won. An eternity later, Steve reclaimed his place on the couch and sipped at his fresh cup.

"Any luck?" she asked.

"No. This time I got a recording saying the number had been disconnected or was not in working order so I guess there's still water in the lines."

He rolled his cup back and forth between his hands. With a frustrated sigh, he put it on the table and stood yet again.

"I'm beginning to feel like a yo-yo. I've never been able to just sit around when things need to get done, so I'm going to try and ride over to my cousin's place. The creek was beginning to recede this morning, so I can probably get across."

A section from one of his letters to his grandmother sprang to Tegan's mind. *You know me, Gran, I never could just wait around for things to happen. That's why I fly jets. Nothing may come of a mission, but I'm up there, flying around, and at least I'm occupied.* It should be no surprise that she understood Steve's reasoning. After all, she was the woman who couldn't sit still unless she had a quilt in her lap to stitch on.

"All right," she said, containing the resurgent spurt of fear that claimed her stomach.

Steve paused as he was leaving, turning to glance at her still form. Her body language was as readable as a billboard—her shoulders were stiff, her fingers almost bloodless as they clenched her cup, her jaw thrust forward defensively.

Not even sure why, Steve found himself saying, "Would you like to come with me?" Stunned by the unexpected words that had just come out of his mouth, he tried to backpedal. "It'll be awfully wet, though. There's still a drizzle. And you've been sneezing . . ."

To his disappointment, Tegan was already moving toward him. "Don't worry. It's just the sniffles."

Trapped by his own invitation, Steve ushered her out the back door, and in no time they were heading their horses out of the gate.

The noontime sun had faded the sky to a pale gray. Tegan supposed it was the best they could hope for. They rode mostly in silence, and she assumed Steve was as lost in the possibilities as she was, but for opposite reasons. Maybe his cousin could shed some light on the subject, but Tegan wasn't sure she wanted to know. These two days until the courthouse was open were a sort of reprieve. She didn't want anything else to worry about if she could help it.

But hiding inside wasn't going to solve anything, either. She could hardly blame Steve for wanting to at least try to get some information.

A long, low rumble of thunder rolled across the sky in the distance. She met Steve's glance, and by unspoken agreement they nudged their mounts into a slightly faster pace. When they reached the creek, Tegan guided her horse next to Steve's and silently watched the swift-moving water.

"It's gone down," Steve said, reporting the obvious. "But I don't think we should try to cross."

Tegan felt a sliver of guilt at her relief and tilted her head forward so that the brim of her hat hid her face in case he looked her way. If Steve had said he was going, she had already decided that she wouldn't take any chances with Dream Chaser. She hated to think of how seriously she would have had to reevaluate her opinion of him if he'd wanted to risk the animals, and themselves.

"I agree. We can try again tomorrow, though."

She followed silently as Steve walked Ghost Dancer along the bank for a time. He seemed to know it was futile but was hoping against hope for a section of low water. When his shoulders sagged, she knew he was ready to admit defeat. She led the way home.

Once more they rubbed the animals down, but Tegan noted that this time the silence was somewhat companionable. She also noticed that the stroke of Steve's brush against Ghost Dancer's hide revealed his frustration. She was afraid it was going to be a very long weekend. Then she reminded herself that she'd distracted him before, and would gladly do so again—not only for her own sake, but because she hated to see anyone as tense and upset as Steve apparently was.

They finished with the horses' grooming and Tegan waited under the small awning while Steve closed the barn behind them. She glanced at the standing water that had turned the grassy patches of the yard into slippery traps and the patches of dirt into mud pits. It was a good thing her boots weren't intended to be worn in public, for the soaked leather would never be pretty again. A cold wind slipped in under her slicker and made her shiver, reminding her just as concretely as her frosty toes that a banked fire was waiting to warm them.

She fought feeling awkward when she took a little slip-step on the treacherous path, and was grateful for Steve's solicitous hand under her elbow. Her mistake came when she tilted her head back to smile her thanks and took her eyes off the ground.

Her boot slid.

She windmilled her arms, yanking her elbow out of Steve's helpful grasp only to grab for him instinctively. His immediate reaction served to help her regain her balance, only to wind up off-balance himself.

His hat tumbled backward as he landed with an ignominious thump in the muddy ooze they had churned up. His hands splashed into the water beside him. Tegan raised her fingers to her mouth to hide her uncharitable smile, trying to restrain the giggle that fought its way to the surface.

It didn't work.

A laugh burst forth in spite of her efforts. Steve raised his face to look at her and then at the handful of wet earth he had just grabbed.

Tegan backed away, still laughing as she held out her hands as if to ward him off. "Now, Steve, you don't want to do that."

"Oh, yes, I do."

"But, you wouldn't do that to an innocent woman, would you?"

Steve was making his way to his feet, never taking his eyes off her.

"An innocent woman? No, I wouldn't. You, however..."

With negotiation failing, Tegan turned to run into the house only to find her waist encircled in a viselike arm. She struggled and found herself twirled around and pulled against his chest in an embrace that made her humor suddenly flee. Her smile faded as she stared into the dark depths of his eyes and watched the playful glint change to something she hadn't seen in a long, long time.

She knew he was going to kiss her.

Time became suspended. She wasn't afraid. In fact, she felt an odd shiver of anticipation as she waited for his mouth to descend to hers. She barely lifted her chin, and they both hesitated as though he were thinking the same thing—this was crazy!

But somehow it didn't matter. A scant second later their lips met, softly, questioningly. Her hands were braced against his chest and even through the layers of fabric and vinyl, she sensed strong, corded muscles.

Suddenly she no longer felt the cold wind whipping around them. She was hot, flushed, as the seeking kiss turned to a welcome hunger.

Tegan felt as though she'd waited for this kiss all her life. She knew the thought was odd, but she didn't care. All that mattered was the velvet feel of his mouth against hers, the strength in his arms as he held her, the warmth he seemed to transfer to her with each shallow, panting breath. He was thoroughly male, and thoroughly real, and it fed her lonely soul.

And as quickly as it had begun, it was over. Steve pulled away and looked deep into her eyes for what seemed like an eternity. The moment was gone and the warm light she had seen was replaced by that constant wariness he wore around him like a mantle, making her wonder if she'd seen it at all. Maybe her eyes were playing tricks on her and she was only seeing something she wanted to see.

They stepped back from each other awkwardly, as though the kiss had stolen all their natural grace. Steve stooped to retrieve his hat and shook most of the muck from his fingers. She hesitated, wary when she saw a hint of a smile return to his handsome mouth.

Before she knew it, he moved back to her and ran the tip of his muddy finger down her nose.

"There, now we're even."

Tegan rolled her eyes, but smiled, as well, her moment of cautious concern swept away by his playful touch. "Let's get inside before we both catch pneumonia."

Steve matched her pace the rest of the way to the house and opened the door for her to precede him. He paused at the threshold, a frown marring his forehead.

"Tegan, I just wanted you to know...I didn't plan that. I usually don't kiss someone the first day I know them."

Tegan escaped into the safety of theory, learned from her time spent reading self-help books after her divorce. It helped her distance herself from the frightening ramifications of this bizarre encounter. It was the only way she could handle the sensations and emotions flooding through her, not the least of which was her fear of the way things were happening too intensely and too fast.

"This is hardly standard procedure for me, either, but I think we both can admit our circumstances are a little unusual. Our emotions are running pretty high, and the situation only telescopes things, making them seem more intense."

"Psych 101?" Steve teased gently. Then he shrugged. "But I think you're right. That's the only explanation for what's happening."

Tegan ignored the fear she recognized behind his smile, and focused all her energy on appearing unaffected by the ensuing silence that was both tantalizing and uncomfortable. It was odd that it seemed the most natural thing in the world to be stripping off her rain gear next to a near stranger, and yet feeling safer than she'd ever felt in her life—especially when that stranger quite possibly had the power to wrest away her heart's dream.

Shaking away the bemusing thoughts, she glanced around the kitchen. "I'm calling dibs on the first shower. Why don't you put some potatoes on to bake for lunch? We'll have a big meal now and eat light at dinner."

"Sounds good." He waited until she was halfway through the living room to shout, "Don't use all the hot water."

There was plenty of hot water—but only one shower. Knowing that he was at least as cold as she was, Tegan hurried through her routine and slipped down the hall to her room, her terry robe about as sexy as her fuzzy slippers. Except that she wasn't trying to be sexy, she reminded herself sternly. That kiss had just been a reaction to a most unusual day. They'd been caught off guard, was all. Under normal circumstances, neither one of them would have given in to a moment like that.

That was the whole problem in a nutshell—these weren't normal circumstances. Her world was topsy-turvy, and her emotions were, as well. She had to admit Steve was a devilishly handsome man, and her romantically starved heart tended to beat a little faster when he looked at her with those deep brown eyes. It was difficult to keep reminding herself over and over of the circumstances that had brought them together, and the possibly devastating outcome. She was a fool to feel anything toward this man except wariness, and maybe anger. She glanced down at the floor as though she could see through the wooden beams and wondered what Steve was thinking.

Steve glanced up at the ceiling. The water had been turned off, and he heard one door open, then another one shut. He supposed that meant she was safely ensconced in her room, but he decided to give it a couple more minutes to be safe. He wasn't sure just what had happened out there in the yard a few minutes ago, but he darn sure wasn't going to invite any more intimate moments. The last thing he needed was to run into her, half-naked from the shower, smelling like the peach-scented shampoo he'd found in the stall earlier this morning. Her skin would be damp from the humidity, her hair would be slicked back and look almost brown—

Shaking his head, he forced himself to stop. If he kept this up, he was going to need his head examined. One thing he was not was sex-starved, and yet here he stood in the middle of the kitchen, fantasizing about a woman he'd just met and how she'd look moments out of the shower.

What he should be concentrating on was how to steel his soft heart against the inevitable pain that was going to come when they got this situation straightened up and he had to help her move her things out.

Four

Tegan shut the door to her room and released a sigh. She'd fought an absurd fear that Steve would catch her in the hallway in her shabby robe, clutching the blow-dryer to her like a weapon.

Not that she should care.

In fact, it shouldn't concern her at all, she told herself sternly as she noted Steve's footsteps, the closing of the bathroom door, and the whoosh of the water being started.

Straightening her posture, she marched to the most convenient outlet and was grateful for the loud whine of the dryer that blocked the sound—the much-too-intimate sound—of someone showering.

Her reactions to this man had to be brought under control! What had happened in the yard earlier was an anomaly. She'd better get it, and get it straight, that he was her enemy and she'd do well to start treating him accordingly. The rules of civil decorum would certainly apply: feed him and offer him clean linen to sleep on, but at all times maintain a sense of caution.

She would not, under any circumstances, dwell on the memory of his lips, firm and hungry against hers, of his arm wrapped around her like a band of flesh-covered steel, of the length of his legs pressed against hers, or the look of barely restrained passion in his warm, brown eyes. And if, by chance, her undisciplined body chose to remember any of those sensations, she would steadfastly refuse to acknowledge the shivers that raced up her limbs to pool in the general region of her abdomen.

From this moment forward she would be cool, collected and impersonal. Polite, but not too friendly. In control, without being autocratic.

Standing, she flipped her now dry hair back, gave it a quick brush, and reached for a clean set of sweats. It wasn't until she caught herself searching the drawer for her least holey pair of socks that she gave herself a mental rap. Holes in her socks or the lack thereof were irrelevant! Who cared if Steve noticed a threadbare place or two? Still, she wished she'd given in to the impulse the last time she'd been at the five-and-dime to pick up a package or two of new ones. But that had nothing to do with Steve.

Only by the strictest application of determination did she get her shoes tied and herself to the door without thinking about him again. Yet when she yanked it open with more force than required, Tegan found herself face-to-face with her nemesis—whom she was *not* thinking about—walking half-naked down the hall.

The already small passageway seemed to shrink, closing in on her with alarming speed.

He'd either forgotten his robe, or didn't use one, because all he had wrapped around his tall, tanned, gorgeous body was a length of terry cloth that hardly seemed adequate. Beads of water still clung to his skin in places, as if he'd only done a haphazard job of drying off. His hair was mussed from a quick toweling, and it was all she could do not to reach up and brush the errant strands from his forehead and wipe away the beads of water with her trembling fingers.

When she realized she was standing in his path, staring like she'd never seen a man without a shirt before, she backed up a step and blushed furiously. "I'm so—" She had to clear her throat to get rid of the squeak. "I'm sorry. I— I was just ... going downstairs."

Steve's eyes were unreadable, but a smile played at the corners of his mouth. "I'll join you shortly."

Nodding, she turned sideways to squeeze past him and hurried to the kitchen, her face still aflame.

She started the chops cooking under the broiler and began the side dishes. A serving of fruit cocktail, a dollop of dairy whip, and a sprinkle of nuts provided the rough semblance of a fruit salad. The broccoli had steamed to a brilliant green, and the potatoes were hot in their silver wrappings.

It suddenly seemed like an odd meal to serve an enemy.

She wondered if the stoneware was too fancy, but then snorted softly. What else could she use? Paper plates? That might be a tad obvious.

As she reached for the iced tea pitcher, she stopped in her tracks. She was doing it again. If she spent half as much physical energy on her quilts as she'd spent in emotional energy in the past twenty-four hours, she could produce at least one a day! Closing her eyes, she counted to ten and took deep, calming breaths. She felt a little more composed by the time Steve appeared in the doorway.

"What can I do to help?" he asked.

She took in his appearance with one swift glance. He had his fingertips thrust into the front pockets of blue jeans that looked like old friends, his blue chambray button-down was tucked in at the waist, and his boots were scuffed. If ever a man looked like an authentic cowboy, Steve did. His clean-cut good looks, his trim, fit body, and his almost-shy smile seemed exactly what a country boy should be.

Collecting herself, Tegan nodded toward the cabinet. "Why don't you put some ice in those glasses? We're almost ready."

Steve took a deep breath. "Smells wonderful."

"Yeah, I guess I'm much too domesticated. I cook, sew, clean. It's really not the nineties thing to admit."

"There you go again. Generalizing about what is politically correct."

They sat down and just as they were putting their napkins in their laps, Tegan was amazed to see Steve drop his head and close his eyes for a brief second. She hadn't seen someone say grace over a meal in...well, in forever.

Steve caught her stare. "What?"

"No-nothing."

"Didn't anyone in your house say grace?"

"Actually, no. Um, we had rather formal dinners. I guess I just didn't expect a pilot...I mean, someone in the service..."

"No one in your family is military."

"How did you know?"

"A lot of praying goes on in the military, Tegan. We say a lot of blessings, we ask for a lot of protection. Not everyone participates, of course, but my grandad would come back from the grave and haunt me if I didn't invoke the Lord's name before a mission or a meal."

"I didn't mean to imply that you were a—"

"Heathen?"

"Now stop that! You're constantly putting words in my mouth. I like that you said a blessing. It just surprised me, okay?"

Steve shrugged away the moment. "So tell me how you became a professional quilter," he asked after swallowing a bite of broccoli.

"I didn't exactly dream about it as I played with my dolls. I was going to be the first woman on the moon." Tegan sat back in her chair and tilted her head sideways. "I guess you came closer to that than I did."

Steve's expression contained a wistfulness that made Tegan feel sad. Then she remembered that from now on Steve would get no closer to the moon than she would.

Clearing her throat, she continued. "Anyway, I started after I got married. I was working fifty hours a week as the branch manager of a title company, and my ex traveled extensively. I wanted something to fill the evenings, and one day my neighbor brought over some of her quilting books. I was instantly hooked. We started a club and had a terrific time."

"And the rest, as they say, is history?"

"Not exactly. As long as this was just a little hobby, the Weasel was fine with it."

Steve choked on a laugh. " 'The weasel'?"

Tegan blushed. "I've called him that for so long I forget to drop it in polite company. His name is Wesley, and I fondly nicknamed him the Weasel during the divorce."

"Pretty nasty?"

"To put it mildly. I was so utterly naive that it took my discovering him in our bed with another woman to catch on that he was not the most faithful man in the world. God, I was stupid."

"You're hardly the first woman who's gone through this scenario."

"Oh, I know. And I think that if I had really loved the Wea—Wes, and he'd loved me, we could have worked things out. The problem was, he had an image of me I couldn't live up to. We had a beautiful home in West Austin and fancy cars. He wanted me to stay home, have children, and be the perfect suburban hausfrau. When we finally had to accept that I wasn't going to be able to get pregnant—we tried for years—he couldn't handle it."

"I'm sorry."

So was she. She had never been able to explain the aching loss, knowing she could never have the children she had hoped for. It had made things worse to know their childless state was because of her. Wes told her that he'd gotten a girl pregnant when he was in high school, but the girl had lost the baby. Since the past proved Wes fertile, the current problem had to lie with Tegan. Few could understand how infertility made a woman feel. There was an overwhelming sense of failure, of being incomplete. It didn't matter that it couldn't be helped, the feelings still hurt. And haunted.

The genuine warmth of his sympathy made her smile.

"You don't need to be. In a strange sort of way, I'm grateful." Tegan chuckled and shook her head. "Would you believe my mother had the gall to tell me to overlook Wes's little indiscretion? She and my father have hardly spoken to me since the divorce. They even dissolved my trust fund, thinking penury would force me to keep my job at the title company, or at least, to 'reconsider my options.'"

"That's terrible!"

Tegan nodded. "You have to understand, appearance is everything to my mother, and she decided she had to show me the error of my ways. She honestly believes that I over-reacted and to this day thinks I was unfair to Wes. My dad stays out of it. He never challenges my mother on anything."

Realizing she was clenching her hands in frustration, Tegan sat back and shrugged. "In the end, it made me make it on my own. Even though there were days I wondered if I'd make enough money to eat, I knew I couldn't go back to the grind of fifty- and sixty-hour work weeks. It was pretty amazing to go from the life-style I had led to near poverty, but I knew there had to be more to life than a big bank account."

"How long has it been?"

"Almost five years." Tegan became lost in her thoughts as she folded her napkin and put it on the table. "You know, the thing that hurt the most wasn't the money. It was that my parents took Wes's side. He still goes over to their house for dinner every few weeks. They've never even been out to see my new house. . . ."

The awkwardness they had managed to avoid was back. She was grateful Steve let the moment pass.

"What doesn't kill us makes us stronger." He grinned and shrugged. "Sorry. I can't seem to stop throwing in a platitude every now and then."

"Wes always wanted me to believe my work was 'just a job.' He never failed to point out that he made the 'real' money. And to him, the quilting was just a hen party, so he laughed when I said I could sell them. Something inside me snapped and I was determined to prove him wrong. Now I can say that my third instruction book is almost finished and I have speaking contracts for the next two years. Not bad for a reformed rich girl."

"Not bad at all," Steve agreed.

"Okay, you've pulled enough out of me. What sent you to the Navy?"

"Jets."

"You certainly are a man of few words! Is that all? Jets?"

A look of deep pain came into his eyes.

"I never knew my father. My mother dropped me off on those very steps—" he tilted his head toward the back door "—when I was eight years old. I used to sit there, waiting for her to come back."

The image his words evoked nearly took Tegan's breath away, and she ached to reach out to touch him. But before she could, he had pulled back again, his words an almost dry recitation of fact, nothing to reveal a wounded, lonely little boy who had turned into a tightly contained man.

"Anyway, I eventually figured out that she wasn't coming back. My grandad was a wonderful man, but he was the product of his time and he didn't cotton to 'waterworks,' as he called it, so I learned not to cry. From the time I was ten years old, I knew I was going to be an aviator and every decision I made from that moment on was based around getting into the Naval Academy."

"My gosh! To be so driven at ten? That's sad."

"It probably kept me out of a lot of trouble. And I realized a dream very few people get to experience. Don't feel sorry for me. I've had a great life."

Tegan felt a moment of discomfort at his use of the past tense. "Can I ask what your plans are now that you can't..."

"Fly? I can. I just can't pull the high G's anymore. As to my plans, I'm not sure. I've still got options, but I haven't made any decisions."

Since she wasn't sure she was ready to learn any more, Tegan pushed her plate away and stood. "I'm going to start the dishes since you did part of dinner."

"You don't have to do that. All I did was wrap potatoes in foil, so I don't think that counts. Just go make yourself comfortable and I'll bring in coffee when I'm done."

A sneeze caught Tegan by surprise before she could answer.

"God bless you," Steve said.

"Thanks." Sniffling, she grimaced. "The last thing I need is the flu. I'm going to find some vitamin C. And I'll take you up on that coffee when you're ready. Cream, light sugar."

After dosing herself with vitamins, Tegan moved to the living room and began a routine that was now automatic. After turning on the stereo to her favorite soft-rock station, she settled into her rocker and set out her supplies. In moments her hoop was positioned comfortably in her lap, her finger was protected with a thimble, and the silver of her needle was flashing through the layers of fabric and batting.

No matter what she was feeling, if she could get herself settled and working on a quilt, everything felt as if it would work out all right.

Steve ran hot water into the sink, watching the bubbles grow around the hard spray. He disdained using the dish-

washer—which seemed anachronistic in the tiny kitchen—
for the few items they'd used. Besides, it would take longer
if he did them by hand. He needed the precious minutes to
reclaim his equilibrium.

He'd tried to stay cool and collected as he'd answered
Tegan's questions, and he'd tried to be honest, as well. But
he wasn't the kind to sit around and talk about his feelings—as Maryanne had pointed out for the thousandth time
as she'd picked up her suitcase and slammed the door behind her.

The phone rang, jarring him out of his reverie. He almost hurried over to answer it, then recalled, for the moment, that it was not his phone. Besides, no one knew he
was here.

Then the decision was out of his hands for he heard Tegan's soft laughter drift in from the other room. Unable to
resist, Steve glanced over the swinging doors and the scene,
in its simplicity, almost took his breath away.

Tegan was sitting in the beautiful wooden rocker by the
fire, a kaleidoscopic quilt in her lap and the phone caught
between her shoulder and ear. She was lit from one side by
the firelight and from the other by the lamp spot-lighting her
work. The picture was so…so peaceful, so inviting, that the
only thing that would have made it perfect would have been
a dog napping on the rug in front of the hearth.

The moment caught him unaware, and Steve couldn't
deny the surge of desire that flooded him. Not sexual, as he
might have expected, but a longing to be a part of this se-
renity, to belong in this picture.

Jerking away from the doorway, he stumbled back to his
chore. Reality slapped him again as he was forced to remember not only that was he not welcome in the little scene
he had witnessed, but also that he could strip the idyllic setting from Tegan's very soul. Her story had touched him
more than he cared to admit, and he wished he could pre-

tend not to understand her very real attachment to this property.

But he couldn't pretend. And if he "won," how hollow the victory would be if he only succeeded in making Tegan as lonely as he was.

Five

Tegan was surprised when the phone rang, but her surprise quickly turned to irritation. The portable receiver was missing from the base unit, and it wasn't on the table next to her rocker. Hurrying over to the other end table, she slapped the button on the base unit to activate the speaker phone and found one of her dearest friends on the other end.

"Enrique, you sweetheart. How are you? Are the storms as bad in Austin as they are here?"

"Not if I'm hearing the weather reports correctly. Are you all right? You sound funny."

Tegan glanced toward the kitchen and heard the sounds of Steve's cleaning. "That's because I have you on the speaker. Hold on a minute."

Looking around, she finally located the receiver between the cushions on the couch. After turning off the speaker, she resettled herself in the rocker and said, "Okay, I'm back. And to answer your question, I'm fine. For the most part."

"What does that mean?"

"Well, besides the fact that I think I'm running a low-grade fever, I might be in some trouble. I really can't talk about it right now except to tell you that the man who inherited the property I bought has shown up. He didn't know about the foreclosure and may have some legal grounds to fight me."

"He's there? With you?"

"Calm down! I'm fine. He's a nice guy, although he's understandably a little angry."

"I'm coming out there—"

"Enrique, no. Besides, we're flooded in. You couldn't get over the creek if you wanted to."

"I told you to get that bridge rebuilt. Now listen, I'll call Angelica—"

"You aren't paying attention to me, as usual. I'm not in any danger. Trust me."

"How can you be so sure? He's a total stranger."

"I know it's odd, but I feel as though I already know this man. I showed you some of the pictures I found. I've read bunches of letters that he wrote to his grandparents." She heaved a sigh. "I realize that hardly seems like enough evidence, but I'm not afraid at all. If I was, I'd tell you in a heartbeat."

Enrique didn't answer.

"Look, it's a moot point. He's been here since last night, so if he was going to do me in, he's already had plenty of time."

"You'd better report in more often."

"As often as the phones will let me," Tegan promised. "I need to let you go. Thanks for checking on me, and tell Angelica I'll call her soon."

With a reluctant goodbye from Enrique, Tegan closed the conversation and returned to her quilting. Enrique and his sister, Angelica, were the best friends anyone could ask for. Angelica was becoming a promising student, and every time she came out, she dragged Enrique with her. Although Angelica wanted to play matchmaker, her hopes were in vain.

Enrique was certainly handsome enough, and it wasn't as though they hadn't tried, but the few dates and kisses Tegan had shared with Enrique had convinced them both that their friendship was much more valuable than romance. Besides, she didn't know what she'd do without Enrique's help with the multitude of chores he willingly lent his broad shoulders to. Which reminded her—she needed to call him about the barn roof soon. She imagined she could hear the loose panels groaning from where she sat and offered a quick prayer that the latest patch job would last through these storms.

The smell of freshly brewed coffee preceded Steve into the room. She smiled as he offered her a cup, sipped, and gave an appreciative sigh. "Perfect."

"Thanks. After trying to drink the swill some of the guys made aboard ship, I learned how to do it myself."

Steve toyed with his spoon and nodded toward the cordless phone at Tegan's elbow. "I didn't notice that earlier."

"That's because the receiver was lost in the cushions. Most of the time I have to use the speaker part to answer it when it rings since I tend to carry the receiver around the house. Half the time I've forgotten—" another sneeze surprised her "—where I put it."

"Bless you. I do that, too. My buddy gave me one of those clap alarm things for my keys one year because he got tired of waiting for me while I searched my apartment. Then I lost the clapper part. And the keys."

Tegan chuckled. "I guess I ought to warn you, then. I order quilting needles by the gross, since I constantly seem to lose them. I wouldn't walk around barefoot."

"Caution duly noted, sir. But don't worry, I'm up to date on all my shots, so I'm pretty safe."

Somehow, I doubt that.

As the conversation lagged, Tegan found herself with her needle poised in her quilt as she watched Steve stare into the fire. She had admitted to herself some time ago that she'd become the tiniest bit infatuated with him, thanks to the photographs and letters. In person, Steve was even more physically compelling. But she knew it was more than his good looks that held her attention. It was the depth of the man. It would have been easy if he had been shallow and self-centered. She would have gladly thrown him out on his proverbial ear.

Clearly, ridding her mind of Steve wasn't going to be that simple. It wasn't just the kiss she couldn't help but recall, though her lips tingled every time she thought of it.

She tried to conjure the memory of Enrique's embraces, as if to prove to herself Steve's kiss hadn't affected her so deeply. She failed. All she could remember of Enrique was a pleasant but not particularly moving experience.

She wished she didn't have to admit that Steve's touch had sent her pulse skyrocketing and she shivered each time she thought about it.

But there was so much more to the problem than a mere kiss. Steve carried an air of confidence, loyalty and dependability that called out to her wary, wounded center. She recognized in him a kindred spirit. While that intrigued her, it also scared her witless.

She'd told Enrique the truth—she was physically safe.

What she hadn't told Enrique was that her heart was in grave danger.

The afternoon progressed quietly but with a notable increase in tension as the hours seemed to drag by. Both Tegan and Steve eyed the clock regularly. Steve's expression had been somber when the radio announcer informed them of a new front moving through the area, and it had turned positively grim when the storm hit a scant fifteen minutes later. The increased thunder and lightning, and the sound of rain falling again in torrential sheets of wind-driven water only added to the strain.

It wasn't until Steve excused himself to retrieve a book that she noticed how tight her shoulders were. She stretched her kinked muscles and resumed work on her quilt before Steve returned.

The domesticity of the scene was not lost on her, despite the taut quality of the atmosphere. Tegan even fleetingly considered how nice it would be to have a man around again, provided she could find one who didn't want to control her, or mold her into some image of his own. She immediately dismissed her wistful thinking. Such a man didn't exist so there was no use dwelling on it, she assured herself, determinedly returning to her task. Yet, after a few stitches, she found herself sneaking glances in Steve's direction again.

Finally acknowledging her futile efforts, Tegan decided to retreat to her bedroom and take a nap. At the least, it would make the day go by faster. She could no longer deny that she indeed had a fever, and it was edging past low-grade with each passing moment. Maybe if she slept, she'd kick this before it turned nasty. Folding her quilt and putting away her notions, Tegan stood and pasted on a polite smile.

"Steve, I—"

Her intended announcement was interrupted by a tremendous crack of lightning followed by a booming roll of thunder. She wasn't sure who jumped farther, but what followed caused them to lock eyes. A groaning and squeaking, as though a huge beast roared, was clear even through the sounds of the storm. Tegan braced herself to feel an impact against the house, and when it didn't come her eyes widened even more in fear.

She and Steve turned simultaneously and ran for the kitchen, yanking on slickers and hats with an almost comic tangle of arms and clothing.

Steve was out the door first. She hadn't even cleared the porch when one glance through the storm-lit yard told her what had happened.

The corrugated metal panel had not listened to her prayers. It now stood braced by the wind, tenuously attached to the roof by a few remaining nails.

Galvanized into action, she raced into the barn with Steve right beside her. She could barely hear the sounds of the agitated shuffling and whinnies of the horses through the deafening pounding of the rain on the tin roof. Water poured through the hole, and Tegan worried about the damage to the loft. The horses would dry off, but bales of wet hay would mold and invite serious trouble.

In the seconds she'd been assessing the damage, she'd attached a carpenter's belt around her waist under her slicker, slipped a hammer into one of the loops, and placed a fistful of nails into the center pouch. She was reaching for her extension ladder when a hand clamped on her shoulder.

"Where do you think you're going?"

Steve's touch and harsh tone jerked her out of her thoughts.

"To fix my roof. Where did you think I was going? For a stroll?"

"It's storming out there."

She couldn't resist a sarcastic smile. "I noticed."

She could feel Steve's anger and she watched with detached amusement as he struggled with himself. She could almost imagine his thoughts. *Stupid woman. Doesn't she know how dangerous it is out there? Should I help or let her get herself killed? It'd almost be easier that way.* Then he'd feel guilty and amend his thinking to a more chivalrous, albeit chauvinistic mode. *I'd better get this done before she hurts herself.*

Steve straightened his shoulders and held out his hand. "Give me the hammer. I'll do it."

"Sorry, Sergeant, I don't take orders from you."

"I'm a captain, not a sergeant, and you *will* give me the hammer."

"We're wasting time. If I'm lucky, that panel is still hanging on by its fingernails out there. Now get out of my way."

"Are you crazy? You can't go up on a barn roof during a storm! Find me a piece of plywood and I'll cover the hole from the inside."

"Look at the roof, Steve. If you throw a piece of plywood up there, all it's going to do is act like a bowl and collect all this storm water. Then it's going to get too heavy and crash down, flooding the whole barn."

"That metal is torn and jagged. Water is still going to get in."

"Yes, but more will run off the roof than through the cracks."

"It's still insane."

"It's still my barn."

The gauntlet had been thrown.

She met Steve's look—a few seconds that felt like a thousand years. She sensed again a battle inside him, but no matter how much he may have wanted to leave her to her own devices, the code he'd grown up with wouldn't let him. The code of the west and the code of the military would not allow him to leave a woman to do a piece of dangerous work by herself. No matter how much he might want to wring her neck.

Steve grabbed the ladder, his eyes daring her to argue, and led the way out of the barn. Leaning it against the roof, he held one side and gestured for her to precede him.

Since this wasn't a skirmish worth fighting, she climbed the rungs already slick from rainwater. She grudgingly acknowledged Steve's strength as he kept the ladder steady.

It's a good thing I'm not afraid of heights, she thought as she carefully maneuvered toward the broken panel. Steve stayed right behind her. Their footing was precarious and their maneuvering treacherous, but they made it to the damaged area.

When the wind snatched her hat away, she foolishly attempted to grab it. Steve's steady hand stopped her dangerous sway and, for a second time, she admitted to herself that she was grateful for his presence. He swept his hat off, intending to give it to her, but the greedy wind took it, too.

Swiping her sodden hair out of her face, she regained her balance. The metal sheet still wavered back and forth in the wind, as though it were trying to make up its mind whether to hang on or go tearing off into the woods like Dorothy's house to Oz.

Steve shouted to her above the wind. "I don't think you can hold this. I'll do it. You nail."

His plan was certainly the most logical, but she still felt a surge of resentment at his authoritarian tone.

Nodding, she fought the urge to assist him—knowing she'd be more harm than help—as Steve struggled to force the panel down. She pounded home nails with quick, powerful strokes. Time became meaningless as she worked her way around the edges of the metal. The adrenaline surging through her system helped her ignore the ice-cold water that ran down her neck.

At last, when the roof was as secure as she could make it, Tegan waited as Steve edged his way back along the roof and down the ladder. She followed him down, but it wasn't until her feet touched the ground that she realized the adrenaline surge that had sustained her was dissipating rapidly. As she stood there, clinging to the rails, her whole body began to tremble. The cold she'd studiously ignored now clawed at her with a vengeance.

Steve pried her hands away. "Come on, Tegan. Let's get inside."

She fought against him as he tried to turn her toward the house. "I ne-ne-need to check on Dream Chaser." She couldn't stop her teeth from chattering. She sneezed violently. Her throat felt like it was on fire.

"They're fine. They aren't even wet. Let's get you inside and dry, and I'll check on them in a bit."

She didn't have any fight left in her. It gave her small comfort to feel a tremor in Steve's hand as he put his arm around her shoulders, although part of her was glad to know that he was not, in fact, Superman after all.

Steve kicked the kitchen door shut behind him as he helped Tegan inside. He stripped his slicker off with weary arms and after a brief argument, helped Tegan out of hers. She was almost collapsing from exhaustion and strain.

She stood there—sodden, freezing—glaring at her hands as though wondering what the malfunction was. Then she glanced around the kitchen as if trying to figure out what to do next. He lifted her chin so that she looked at him.

"Tegan," he said slowly and calmly, "we're going to go upstairs now. You're going to take a hot bath and then get into bed. I'll bring you up something hot to drink in a minute."

She shook her head, but he sensed it was not a denial of his suggestion but an attempt to clear her thoughts. "'Kay."

Steve put his arm around her once more and held on as she began to walk with exaggerated care toward the living room. He was unprepared when she clutched at his supporting arm and came to a sudden stop.

"You're cold," she said accusingly.

"I know, Tegan. I'm going to change, too."

They managed another lurching step before Tegan halted again. This time a coughing fit bent her over. When she caught her breath, she straightened and turned her head toward him. "You can't take a bath with me."

Steve was too startled by her words and his body's instant response to speak. Then he saw that her eyes had taken on a feverish gleam. Her cheeks were flushed red with heat despite her shivering body.

"All right," he assured her, keeping his voice soothing. "I won't. Come on, here we go."

The trip up the stairs proved interesting. By the time they reached the landing, Steve knew that although the bath was a good idea to get her warm, it would be a logistical nightmare for him. Besides, if he left her alone, she'd probably fall asleep and drown herself.

Quickly changing the plan, Steve guided Tegan to her room.

Tegan put her hand on the doorjamb. "I thought I was taking a bath."

"Change of orders. We're going to get you dried off and into warm jammies. Then, it's into bed."

Tegan's forehead furrowed as she took in the new instructions. "I don't wear pajamas."

The image of just what she did—or didn't—wear to bed did more to warm him up than any blanket ever would.

His arm tightened around her. "A nightgown?"

Her face cleared. "Okay."

When he started unbuttoning her blouse, Tegan batted his hands away. "I can do it."

"Tegan, you're freezing. We've got to get you dry."

She looked at him with narrowed eyes. "I can do it," she argued through her teeth.

He looked at her warily before shrugging. "Okay, but if you're not ready for bed when I come back from changing, I'll do it for you."

When Tegan nodded, he reluctantly left her to get undressed. By the time he reached his room, he felt every inch of ice-cold clothing that was plastered against his skin. Stripping out of his clothes, he gratefully pulled on a sweat suit. Fresh, dry socks felt heavenly against his freezing toes. While drying his hair, he thought about Tegan, and started plans for a long night.

She had probably been working on that fever all evening but hadn't been aware of it. He remembered how her sneezing had increased over the day, but he hadn't given it much thought earlier. Spending an hour out in the freezing rain on the barn roof certainly had not helped. Now it was obvious that she was in for a rough bout with the flu.

And strangely, or maybe not so strangely, he was glad he would be here to help her. He'd nursed himself through this stuff before and knew it was no fun being sick and trying to take care of yourself. From what he'd gleaned, it seemed like Tegan deserved a little pampering.

Dropping his towel, Steve headed for her bedroom, scolding his errant pulse for racing when he considered what he might find just two doors down.

Six

Steve wasn't sure if he was relieved or disappointed to find Tegan fully concealed in a faded flannel nightgown. He stopped for a second in the doorway, exasperated with himself. *A sick woman in flannel should not look desirable.* Tegan obviously didn't know the rules.

She lay on the end of her bed—on top of her quilt. With her knees curled to her chest, she had one arm wrapped around her waist while her other hand rested under her cheek. Her hair was fanned out on the bed, as though she'd lifted the honey-gold mass to get it off her neck and then let it rain behind her.

Reluctant to disturb her, but knowing she had to get under the covers, he moved closer and shook her shoulder gently.

"Tegan, wake up."

She stirred, nodding her head. "'Kay," she said sleepily, but her body remained uncompliant.

"Tegan—"

He started to shake her again but decided to take another course of action. Folding back the covers as much as possible, he simply walked to the end of the bed and scooped her up into his arms.

She automatically wrapped her arms around his neck. When she snuggled into his shoulder, Steve found his breath caught in his chest. He carried her only a few steps, but that was enough contact to leave his arms trembling.

He laid her down and pulled the covers around her. As soon as she hit the sheets, Tegan hugged a pillow to her chest and went to sleep. He placed his hand on her neck to gauge her fever. She felt hot, but she wasn't burning up. Yet.

Spying a control for an electric blanket, Steve turned it on low. He wanted her to stay warm, but not too hot. Her body was already doing that on its own. With her settled for the moment, he hurried downstairs to fix himself something hot to drink and to see what he could find to treat Tegan. He hoped she had some aspirin in the house, and he'd get her to drink as much as possible during the night.

He glanced at the clock and shook his head. Only six o'clock? It already felt like the dead of night. After one last mad dash to keep his promise and check on the horses, he returned to the kitchen to fortify himself with two big sandwiches and a cup of hot chocolate.

For Tegan he fixed some chicken broth he found in the pantry. He filled a carafe with a batch of tepid broth, and another with cool water, remembering enough first aid to know that whatever she took in would need to be of a moderate temperature. Her system was having enough trouble without throwing boiling soup or ice-cold water on her stomach.

It would probably be a long night, and if he didn't want to succumb to the tightening he felt in his own chest, he knew he'd better take care of himself. He headed back upstairs and put the tray on Tegan's dresser. He located a thermometer and coaxed her into keeping it under her tongue until he could get a read on it.

One hundred and two. Not as bad as he'd thought, at least.

After popping down a couple of aspirins himself, he coaxed Tegan to take a dose, and then tried to get as comfortable as possible in the chaise lounge that was lovely to look at but much too short for his frame. Resigned, he covered himself with another of Tegan's master quilts and tried to rest. If her bout with the flu ran true to form, she'd start tossing and turning in the next several hours and then would come the cold sweats.

For a moment his callous side reared its ugly head and asked him why he was being so attentive. She wasn't going to die—she just had the flu. She could take care of herself. In fact, if he wasn't there, she'd have to take care of herself, right? Maybe this would help prove to her that she had no business trying to run the place by herself. Maybe this would convince her to go back to Austin.

His own thoughts irritated him. What little he knew of Tegan assured him that she would never buckle under so easily. And, of course she'd pull through, regardless of whether he helped her or not. Her survival wasn't the question. His humanity was.

These past couple of years he'd found himself becoming more withdrawn, colder in nature. He'd started to believe that life was going to be just one stretch of hours blending into another. Without his career, without his jet, what was it all about?

He hadn't liked what he'd seen in himself. In fact, that was what had prompted this very trip home. It wasn't that he was excessively angry—it was that he wasn't excessively anything. No highs, no lows, just a monotonous pattern of nonreaction. His first big clue had been his lack of concern when a buddy had been forced civilian during the last round of the Reduction in Force. Everyone worried about being RIF'd, but the most he could muster for Dean, his best friend, had been "Bad break, dude. Keep in touch."

Maybe it was a stretch to link these two events, but if playing nursemaid made him feel connected, it hardly seemed like a crime.

Or maybe you're assuaging your conscience for when you kick her out, that nasty little voice added.

Refusing to dwell on that disturbing thought, Steve resettled himself and tried to grab what rest he could before the "fun" began.

It started at about two o'clock in the morning. Tegan's thrashing as she threw off her covers startled him from his sleep. Her gown and bedclothes were soaked. She was mumbling in her sleep, alternately clutching the sheet to her and shaking, then throwing them off and breathing like she was running a marathon.

Steve located clean clothes first and coaxed Tegan out of her wet ones. He was glad to find that his pulse behaved as he took in the physical beauty of her body while he helped her into a dry nightgown. He towel-dried her hair and then wrapped her in a blanket before settling her in the chaise. With a tired sigh, he remade her bed.

He successfully coaxed her to take a good bit of the broth, and after it looked like it was going to stay down, he dosed her again with aspirin. One last transfer back, and the two of them were in their original positions.

The cold chills hit next. He could only stroke her face and make soothing noises as she curled in on herself and shivered. He periodically took her temperature, pleased that it never passed 103°. He wasn't sure how, but if it had climbed any higher he'd have found a way over that creek to get her to the hospital, if he'd had to swim to do it.

Thankfully, once the chills subsided, a peace settled over her body. An exhausted peace, to be sure, but she seemed past the worst. After one last dose of medicine, he left her alone to sleep.

As he passed Tegan's sewing room, he stopped. His desire to go inside to see her inner sanctum was so strong it was almost a compulsion. The door was ajar, so with only the slightest bit of guilt at going in uninvited, Steve turned on the light and stepped inside.

The room was a study in organized chaos. To his tired eyes the piles of colored fabric were almost unbearable to look at. Bolts of cloth lay atop each other like fallen dominoes. Swatches were pinned to a cork board and his untrained eye couldn't begin to imagine how she was going to combine pink, orange and lime green.

How could someone so messy create such precise masterpieces, sew such tiny stitches, be so detail-oriented? Maybe it was the very contrast that made up her talent. He didn't know and didn't even try to hazard a guess.

But this room, as no other in the house, bore her stamp. Although she had clearly placed her imagination into the decoration of the house, this room contained her soul. A drafting table took up one corner and he glanced at the graph paper clipped under the swing-arm lamp. He was no quilter, but the design she'd drawn appealed to him—clean lines, yet with a sense of balance, of harmony. The image came to him of what it felt like to be above the clouds, doing Mach 1, the radio in his helmet mostly silent. All he could hear was his own breathing, and that sounding harsh and foreign because of his mask.

He stepped closer to her cutting table and glanced down. A ruler lay juxtaposed to the edge, next to a pizza cutter. Then he realized it was actually a round razor. The newest revolution in scissors, he supposed. He reached out to the length of cloth that had been spread over the flat surface, thinking that he couldn't have stopped himself from running his fingers over the soft green fabric if he'd tried.

Was this what Tegan had felt as she'd gone through his pictures and letters? If so, he now understood her discomfort. This glimpse inside someone's private world was so...intimate. And to be there uninvited was improper. He could blame his intrusion on exhaustion, he guessed. Or maybe he needed to know more about her because of her absolute trust in him while he'd cared for her. He'd taken enough psychology courses to know that if she had felt threatened or scared, no matter how sick she was, she would have fought him to her last ounce of strength.

Shaking his head, he glanced at the far wall and saw an oversize calendar. Someone named Enrique had had a birthday last week. Angelica was due for a lesson. One caption reminded Tegan to prepare for a lecture. Another reminded her of a deadline for her manuscript.

The other wall was full of pictures, mostly of women, some in groups, some individual shots. Several held finished quilts and pride radiated from their faces. In a frame next to her sewing machine, Tegan smiled at him from a snapshot. She was flanked by a Hispanic man and woman. Whoever the guy was, the dark-headed woman on Tegan's other side had to be his sister. He wondered if the man was Enrique.

A flash of jealousy caught him unaware.

Glancing away from the picture, he took in the room again.

She belonged here. His curiosity was satisfied, but he'd only increased his dilemma.

Too tired to work it out now, Steve turned away and shut off the light. Making his way to his bed, he dropped onto the mattress with a groan, expecting to fall asleep the second his head hit the pillow. Instead he found himself smiling in the darkness with a sense of relief that Tegan was going to be fine.

And a sweet sense of satisfaction when he'd expected to feel nothing at all.

It was a little frightening, come to think about it. To realize he'd been coasting along, merely reacting to the events in his life these last long months, and now to get a taste of the old spark back was a lot to consider. Could something as simple as taking care of someone awaken his desire to be proactive instead of reactive?

He didn't have a chance to answer himself. He was asleep.

* * *

Tegan awoke feeling like someone had stuffed cotton down her throat, was sitting on her chest and using her head for a bongo drum. Opening her eyes carefully, she took in the destruction around her room. She wished she didn't, but she remembered most of what Steve had done for her last night. Rolling her head back, she closed her eyes and retreated into another few minutes of sleep.

A cool hand on her forehead roused her again. She forced her eyes open but she already knew Steve was sitting on the bed beside her, his hip pressed against hers as he leaned over her.

"Hey, Sleeping Beauty. How do you feel?"

"Like I've gone twenty rounds with George Foreman."

"I think you lost."

"Thanks. That makes me feel much better."

"Well, how about this, then?"

She glanced at the glass of apple juice and two aspirin he offered. "You certainly know how to woo a girl, Steve."

"When you're back in fighting form, I'll revert to my usual charming self. Until then, take advantage of me."

She managed a creditable smile and lifted one eyebrow. "Hmm, I'll have to give that some thought."

It was torture to swallow the medicine, but she felt better almost immediately. Even though she knew the effect was psychosomatic, she wasn't going to argue.

Her head itched. When she reached to scratch it, her humor faded and she felt a growing discomfort. "I must look like death warmed over."

"Actually, you look beautiful. Pale, but beautiful."

Whatever she had expected him to say, that was not it. A caustic retort or another cute remark, maybe. A glance into his eyes told her he wasn't joking.

She was not ready for this.

"Thanks, but I feel in desperate need of a shower. If you'll excuse me . . ."

Steve seemed reluctant to obey, but finally conceded. As he left, he picked up armfuls of things that needed to be returned downstairs. Something about the room twitched at the back of her mind, but she couldn't put a finger on it. Shrugging, she accepted that she should stop Steve from cleaning up, but she wisely decided to conserve what little energy she had.

By the time she climbed into the hot shower, washed her hair and rinsed her body, she was about worn out. It took her determined effort to get into clean clothes and back under the covers before giving in to another rest period. As her eyes drifted shut, she thought she heard the phone ring, but was too tired to care.

Steve hurried to catch the phone on the first ring. He had a flash of hope that it would be Billy. Then he remembered that his cousin didn't know he was here.

"Who's this?" a deep, male voice asked.

"Who are you trying to reach?" Steve returned. Wrong number, probably.

"I'm trying to reach Tegan McReed. Who are you?" the caller demanded again.

"Steve Williams. Tegan's unavailable. Can I take a message?"

"Why is she unavailable?"

Steve was beginning to get a little angry. "Listen, buddy, if you don't tell me who you are, I'm not going to tell you another thing."

"My name is Enrique Esquivel. I'm a friend of Tegan's. A very good friend."

Steve almost smiled at Enrique's tone. In a moment of twisted humor, he almost wished Enrique a belated happy birthday.

"Tegan's got the flu. She's asleep at the moment."

"I want to talk to her."

The challenge in Enrique's voice stiffened Steve's shoulders.

"I said, she's asleep."

"If she's hurt—"

"Listen, Enrique, Tegan's fine. She's just sick. I'll have her call you when she gets up. Until then, you'll have to be satisfied."

"You just keep in mind, fly-boy, that I'm checking you out. I'll be there as soon as I can get across that creek."

"You do what you need to do, man. We'll be here."

Steve replaced the receiver after Enrique hung up. He couldn't help but wonder how far Tegan's relationship went with this Enrique. His mind flashed to the picture he'd seen and if that was the same person, this guy had the dark, Latin look that he knew appealed to women. Some of his buddies had that look and the ladies seemed to fall all over them. Even though Tegan didn't seem the fall-all-over-them type, he couldn't stop the question from repeating in his head.

And so what if she was involved with someone? What business was it of his?

None, except that he didn't like being threatened.

Stuffing down his reaction, Steve headed for the stairs to check on her. She needed to eat soon.

When Steve yanked back her curtains an hour or so later, Tegan found the answer to what she couldn't place before. Sunshine! It had been peeking beneath the curtains earlier. Now it streamed through her window and flooded the room with a golden glow.

"It's stopped raining!"

"Brilliant deduction, Watson."

"Oh, hush. I'm just so excited. I thought the sun was never going to shine again."

"Hmm, if that's all it takes, I'll have a talk with Mr. Sun."

She cocked her head and stared at him. When she finally understood the joke, her eyes opened wider. Steve was certainly in a playful mood this morning. Granted, she hadn't known him long, but that seemed out of character. Maybe this was the real Steve and the moody, angry man who had burst in on her was the anomaly.

She wasn't ready for him to change personas yet. She was hardly used to the first one; she certainly wasn't prepared to deal with a new one.

"Stop that," she said sullenly.

"Stop what?" he asked, genuinely surprised.

"Being so nice."

Steve had been piling glasses and tissues onto the tray. He stilled his hand and looked at her. "I beg your pardon?"

"You're being too nice. It makes me nervous."

"I wasn't aware that I'd been that much of a bully up to now."

"You haven't. It's just you seem so . . . chipper."

It was almost as if she'd turned off a switch.

"Sorry. I won't make that mistake again."

Chagrin and regret flooded through her. "Steve, I—"

"Someone named Enrique called. I told him I'd pass along a message."

With that, Steve was out the door carrying the loaded tray.

Shaking her head, she reached for the phone to return Enrique's call. She was surprised by the anger in his voice. It took a lot of fast talking to convince Enrique to stay home until she needed him. He finally promised to wait until she asked before he came out.

Forcing herself out of bed, she ran a brush through her hair and put on slippers before following Steve downstairs. She found him in the living room, channel surfing with the satellite remote.

She settled into her chair and covered herself with a lap quilt. "The weather channel is on—"

"I know, I found it."

"Steve, I'm—"

"Are you hungry?" he asked as he tossed the remote onto the cushions and stood. "I was just about to find something to eat."

"Yes, thanks. Steve—"

"I'll call you when it's ready."

Again, he was out of the room before she could voice an apology.

Men! Could she help it if she wasn't in her peak form at the moment? She was weak and tired and grouchy. She was sorry she had barked at him, but the jerk wouldn't stay still long enough for her to apologize. What did he want from her?

Annoyed at her thoughts, Tegan calmed herself. She was in no position to berate him when she was the one acting out-of-sorts. It was just that . . . well, she felt vulnerable. Steve was a threat. Not physically, of course, but in a way that had the potential to hurt her much deeper. Every time she sensed her guard slipping, it scared her. She had learned in her marriage to strike first when she was wary. She thought she'd trained herself out of the habit, but maybe it was too deeply ingrained.

She jumped in fright when Steve's shadow fell over her. He was offering her a lap tray with toast, oatmeal, and juice on it.

"I'm going to go exercise the horses and check out the barn. It'll be a while before I get back."

He had almost made it through the kitchen when her voice stopped him.

"Steve?"

"Yeah?"

"Thank you."

A long pause ensued.

"You're welcome."

The door slammed.

Slowly munching her toast and jelly, Tegan wondered again at the strange man who had exploded into her life. Snatching the remote, she began her own random sampling of the available channels.

Seven

Bundled head to toe in warm clothes and boots, Tegan climbed into the passenger seat of Steve's Jeep. The weatherman had promised it would warm up by the afternoon, but the morning was still chilly. She tried to blame the trembling in her fingers on the cold, but she knew it was a lie, for the same trembling had settled in her stomach. She glanced around and couldn't even enjoy the brilliant sunshine that bathed the yard and turned the lingering drops into crystal prisms. She was usually able to revel in the sharp, clean smell of the cold air, but not this time.

Steve slammed his door and settled himself in the driver's seat. His motions lacked the fluidity of his usual grace, her biggest clue that Steve was equally as nervous. Of course, his face remained impassive.

Her stomach did another little lurch as she looked at him. She wished, for the hundredth time, that he was just a little less handsome, just a little less chivalrous, just a little less...undeniably male. She didn't like the stirrings that wound around inside her when he looked at her with those huge brown eyes.

With a little coaxing, the engine turned over. The sound forced her out of her trance and she concentrated on the drive as they made their way toward Johnson City. And, she hoped, to some answers.

She had tried to tell Steve last night how grateful she was that he had waited an extra day to go into town. She still felt guilty for believing he would go ahead without her. To her surprise, he had paused after her announcement that the flu had taken too much out of her for her to try to make a long day in town. Then he'd said that it wouldn't be fair for him to do this "behind her back." So he'd offered to wait until this morning, and she hadn't hesitated to take him up on his offer.

The more she thought about yesterday, the more jumbled her emotions became. It had been more than his brusque response to her thanks that had told her how anxious Steve had been. His behavior had been clear. While she had stayed snuggled up on the couch, he had spent the day prowling—taking care of the horses, working on the barn roof, serving her hot drinks and soft foods, and trying to call his cousin. Tegan also realized she had been strangely grateful for her lassitude—it was the perfect excuse to stay out of his way.

As the day had stretched into night, Steve had become more withdrawn. She'd wished he had ranted and raved; that way she could have built up a more effective resentment toward him. Instead her heart had gone out to him. She could only guess at the depth of his fear.

No, that wasn't true. She knew exactly what his fear level was—identical to hers.

Again this morning Steve had been unable to contact his cousin. He had hurried her through a light breakfast and into the Jeep, where she now sat holding on to the strap to keep herself seated as they rocked and jerked over the road, and finally over the bridge.

The ride took just over thirty minutes, but it seemed interminable. When he pulled into a parking space at the courthouse, they sat in awkward silence. Eventually, with a glance in her direction and a strained smile, Steve got out.

He wasn't surprised Tegan had already jumped down by the time he made his way around the back of the Jeep. He had intended to help her, but her eyes and body language told him that she didn't need any more cosseting. With a nod to acknowledge that the message was received, he led the way inside the red brick annex situated across from the historic limestone courthouse. Their footsteps echoed loudly in the hallway. Steve shook away the absurd thought that the sound was ominous.

He wished he could shake away his thoughts of Tegan as easily. He had pretended not to, but he had been aware whenever her gaze had lingered on him in the Jeep. Every time those luminous blue eyes swept over him, his pulse raced in answer. He wanted to rip the gloves off his hands and the scarf from her head so he could wrap his fingers in the liquid gold cascade of her hair. He wanted to kiss her and tell her everything would be all right.

But he couldn't do that. Because he didn't know if it would be true.

They entered the tax assessor's office and moved to the counter. Someone had made a half-hearted attempt to decorate by taping up some cutouts of a cute witch and black cat but it was a blond woman with a distinct tint of pink in her bouffant hairdo who commanded his attention. Steve thought the lady had that sprayed-and-lacquered look that could have been done at the beauty shop yesterday or a week ago—there was no way to tell.

It reminded him fiercely of his grandmother and the way she'd kept her long hair braided and wrapped around her head during the day. One evening he had been lying across her bed, talking to her while she'd brushed it. He'd asked her why she didn't cut it like all the other grandmothers, and she'd smiled her patient, tender smile and said simply,

"Because your grandpa likes it long." That had been reason enough for her. He hadn't understood until many years later the desire to do something for someone else simply because it would please them.

The woman looked at Steve for a moment before recognition dawned in her eyes.

"Why, you're Mr. Williams's boy, aren't you?" the woman asked as though Randall Williams were still alive and selling two-by-fours just down the street. "Steve, isn't it?"

"Yes, ma'am," Steve affirmed, nodding politely as he removed his hat.

"We haven't seen you around here in a month 'o Sundays. How in the world have you been?"

"Fine, thank you."

"My name is Harrietta Parsons. You probably don't remember me, but your grandma and I used to be in the same quilting bee. Of course, I was just a young thing, then. We used—"

"Mrs. Parsons, we're here—"

"Oh, call me Retta. Everyone does. Listen, we sure were sorry to hear about your granddaddy passin'. But I told Onellma Dickson as soon as I heard your grandma had taken ill that it wouldn't be long before your granddaddy followed. Those two were somethin' else. Why—"

"I'm sorry," Steve interrupted, smiling to soften his tone, "I don't mean to be rude, but we need to find some information."

The woman's cheeks flushed and she placed a hand over her heart. "I'm sorry. I didn't mean to carry on so. I mean, it's been what? Over ten years now. I haven't seen you since the funeral and it was just such a surprise. I read in the *Stars and Stripes*—" The woman stopped herself and turned a darker shade of pink. "I'm doin' it again, aren't I? Well, I'll just stop that foolishness. What can I do for you folks?"

Steve handed her an old tax receipt. "I have a problem with the taxes on this parcel. It seems the money may have been misapplied."

"Well, that's no problem," Retta beamed. "If you have your canceled checks or receipts from this office, we can straighten things out in no time."

Steve cleared his throat. "That's where the problem lies. I don't have the receipts, and I was hoping we could get some information from the computers."

"I'm afraid there's not much I can tell you from my computer. All I can do is tell you how much the taxes are, and if they're paid, things like that. I'll be happy to look it up for you, though."

Retta took the slip and keyed in the numbers. She read the screen, looked at the receipt in her hand, and then over at Steve.

"I'm sorry, but this property is owned by a Tegan Mc-Reed."

"I'm Te—" Tegan tried to interject.

"That's what we're trying to clear up," Steve interrupted, forcing the impatience out of his voice. "My property was auctioned for delinquent taxes and I'm trying to find out where the payments which should have been applied to this property are."

"How long has it been?" Retta asked. "Since the property was sold, I mean."

"Just over two years."

Retta made a clucking noise. "That's a shame. You only have two years to file an objection." Her face brightened. "But you know, you really ought to go over and talk to Judge Ohlman. He and your granddaddy were good friends. I bet he'd help fix it for you."

"How could he do that?"

Steve heard an edge of panic in Tegan's voice, and felt an answering tightness in his own chest.

"Oh, honey, I just bet that because Steve's been away, with the military and all, that he could file suit and ask for an extension to appeal due to extenuating circumstances."

Steve tried to smile again, thinking that if indeed Judge Ohlman did "fix" anything, Retta had also given Tegan the ammunition to fight it. "Thanks, Retta. I'll check into it."

He put a hand under Tegan's elbow to lead her out. Her arm trembled beneath her jacket.

Tegan stopped in the hallway. "What do we do now?"

Steve shrugged. "Find Billy, I guess." He ran his fingers though his hair with an impatient jerk. "Tegan, I'm—"

"Don't." She shook her head as she crossed her arms. "Don't say you're sorry. This is only the beginning and we both know it. Let's get on with what we need to do without saying things we'll both regret."

He nodded sharply and led the way outside, his emotions a jumble of fear and an absurd pride at the way Tegan contained herself. He had no right to be proud of her, but he was.

"There's no use in trying to call Billy again, so let's head over to his place and see if he's home." When she agreed, a thought occurred to him. "Are you getting hungry? Maybe we should eat first."

Tegan shrugged one shoulder and rubbed the bridge of her nose. "I'm not hungry, but I could use a cup of coffee."

They drove the couple of blocks to Ada's Place, and Steve couldn't stop the memories that assailed him. He led Tegan to a table and let them wash over him.

For all that had changed, he could be ten years old again. The pictures on the walls were the same, the smells of cooking oil and strong coffee were the same, the sounds of dishes clanking in the kitchen were the same; all that was missing was Ada saying—

"Good Lord Amighty, look what the cat dragged in!"

Steve smiled before he turned and saw her. Her hair was exactly the same shade of red he remembered, she still wore gardenia perfume, and the only hint that she'd aged in the last twenty years was the increase in number of laugh lines around her mouth and eyes.

He'd had a mad crush on her when he was ten and she was thirty-something. Now that he was thirty-something and she was... well, it didn't matter. Ada would always be special to him. From the first time his grandad had brought him here, Ada had teased him like he was "growed up," and she'd made a little boy laugh.

"I had a hankering for flapjacks, Ada. And I knew the best place to come."

"I swear you'd better know, young man." Ada turned her eyes to Tegan and included her in the friendly greeting. "And who's this pretty little girl you got with you?"

"Ada, this is Tegan McReed. Tegan, meet Ada..." Steve looked up. "Ada, I don't know your last name!"

"Wouldn't matter if you did, 'cause it's changed four times since the last time you set foot in here. It's Butler, for now."

Steve laughed and noted that Tegan smiled politely and offered her hand. Ada shook it and then grabbed the pencil she'd stashed among the red curls. "So, what do you folks want this morning?"

Steve found his appetite had returned and put in an order to back it up. Tegan ordered coffee, and finally some toast and jelly—more to quiet Ada's horrified objections than because she was hungry. He decided he didn't care what made her eat, as long as she did. She was too pale and too thin from her recent bout with the flu.

Once the table was piled with the food he had ordered, he dug in with relish. Nobody made grits like Ada, that was for sure.

"Interesting place," Tegan said, glancing around.

"You haven't been in before now?" Steve asked, surprised.

"I don't get into town much. I've looked at a building a couple of blocks over, thinking I might open a shop, but I haven't made up my mind yet. I'm also considering something in Wimberley.''

''I'm sure you'd get plenty of business—''

The aroma of gardenia preceded the voice. ''How're you folks doing? More coffee?''

Both said yes and Ada poured. ''Steve, I'm real sorry to hear about Billy. It's just such a shame.''

Steve felt his muscles clench and suddenly he lost his appetite. Putting his fork slowly against his plate, he met Ada's glance. ''I don't understand.''

Ada's eyes grew round. ''You didn't know? Oh, my God. I've done it now.''

''Ada, please. Tell me what you mean.''

''Well, a couple years ago the IRS took his property. It woulda killed his daddy. Your uncle was such a proud man. I'm glad he wasn't here to—''

''Wait! Why—''

''It was the gambling, Steve. Everybody in town knew about it. Then the drinking got worse and, well, you can guess the rest.''

Steve swallowed an oath. ''Where is he?''

''Last I heard he was shacking up with some girl in Marble Falls. You know Billy—he always fancied himself quite the ladies' man. I think he keeps in touch with the Faulkner boy, if you want to give Kenneth a call. He could give you Billy's number, I'm sure.''

''Thanks, Ada,'' he said, forcing a taut smile.

She put a solicitous hand on his shoulder. ''I really am sorry. I wouldn't have brought it up, but I thought you, of all people, would know.''

Steve patted her fingers. ''It's all right. I've been out of touch for a long time. Too long, obviously.''

''I'm sure Billy'll be glad to see you.''

Somehow, I doubt it. ''Yeah. Thanks again.''

Steve alternately sipped at his coffee and ran his fingers through his hair. He appreciated Tegan's patient silence. He didn't think he could talk about it yet.

He was uncomfortable with the realization that in his heart he had known all along something was wrong. Terribly wrong. That phone recording was no error. *Water in the lines, my foot!* And he hated admitting his own need to deny the truth had kept him from having the operator check the number.

It was just another tally in his column of selective denial. The score-keeping had started the first year he hadn't received the tax receipts, and he'd made up reasons why they hadn't come. The notches had increased with each sporadic phone call from Billy and every excuse Steve had swallowed. The total was quickly becoming more than he could choke down, though, and he had no one to blame but himself. Good God! The local waitress knew more than he did!

Tegan's voice brought him back. "Steve? Are you ready to leave?"

"Yeah, but I need to make a phone call. Would you take care of the bill?" He handed her a twenty and the slip of paper containing Ada's illegible shorthand.

When he met Tegan at the door to the diner a few minutes later, Steve had his answer. Kenneth did indeed know where Billy was and had gladly provided the address and phone number. Unwilling to conduct his meeting with Billy either over the phone or in public, he'd made up his mind to get Tegan home and head to Marble Falls.

Tegan continued to leave Steve alone with his thoughts as they drove back. After his announcement that he was taking her home and then heading back out, there really wasn't much to say. She could hardly invite herself to a meeting that would no doubt be uncomfortable.

She tried to sort out the information she'd received today and couldn't stop a surge of hope that made her feel ashamed. It certainly looked like Cousin Billy had royally messed things up for himself, and by all accounts for Steve, as well. Somehow she doubted the trip to Marble Falls would reveal any canceled checks or missing receipts.

With that thought again came the mixed feeling of hope and guilt. The little voice of pessimism also reminded her of the idea Retta had planted in both their brains.

She had the sudden vision of a courtroom, strains of "Hail the Conquering Hero" playing as Steve walked in and took his place at the plaintiff's table. She was on the witness stand, being grilled by a malevolent attorney. She would be painted as a heartless hussy who had come into town and taken advantage of their local, God-fearing, red-blooded, American Navy pilot. And worse, she was a— there would be great gasps around the courtroom at this point— *Yankee*.

She could almost feel the censorious eyes turning on her, hear the unspoken invectives. She would never get the chance to explain she'd only been born a Yankee. She'd lived all her life right here in Texas—

Stop that!

They arrived home and Steve accompanied her into the house. He disappeared upstairs for a moment after accepting her offer to make him a thermos of coffee. When he came back down, he stopped beside her as she leaned against the counter, waiting for the brew to finish dripping.

She couldn't take her eyes off the coffeemaker. The drip of each drop as it splashed into the decanter sounded like a crash. Her fingers trembled on the drainboard.

Steve brought his hand up, as though he were going to touch her shoulder, then slowly dropped it again. She forced herself to look at him, and she knew what was coming. It felt just like it had out in the yard the first time, the moment stretching into forever, the confusion and desire in his eyes, the matching emotions in her own.

It was insanity revisited, and she could no more deny the lure of its call than she could stop her heart from beating. The small portion that remained of her rational mind told her she would regret this, that she should run as far and as fast as she could. But the rest of her, pulled back and forth between fear and desire, had no more fight left.

"Steve, we shouldn't—"

"Tegan, this is crazy—"

The words were lost as their mouths met and melded. Tegan sighed as Steve traced her lips with his tongue and pressed against her, gathering her body to him as his kiss deepened.

Something flared like the lightning recently passed. Their fusion became desperate, hard and demanding. Tegan clutched at Steve's shoulders and he wound his fingers into her hair. His body was a magnet, irresistible, pulling her length against his.

She didn't care, didn't want him to stop when his mouth became a bruising force against hers. His tongue demanded entrance and she obeyed willingly, recklessly. She gave as well as she took until she felt light-headed.

A whimper escaped when Steve tore his mouth away. She was reassured when he rested his forehead against hers, struggling to breathe much like she was. . . .

"I have to go," he finally said as he stepped away.

She could only nod.

Her whole body trembled as she watched Steve turn on his heel and stride out the door. She wanted to shout at him to wait, to take her with him.

Or better still, not to go at all.

But it was time for this to be over, this lifetime that had taken place in three days. With a sigh she closed the door and went into the living room to call Enrique.

It wasn't until she brought the receiver up to her ear and brushed her cheek with her hand that she realized she was crying.

Eight

Steve spent the entire drive to Marble Falls berating himself for being seven kinds of a fool. What had gotten into him, kissing Tegan like that?

What had gotten into him, he admitted, was the feeling of certain dread that had settled into his bones that once he talked to Billy, his relationship with Tegan would take a radical shift. He had denied the overwhelming need to touch her and kiss her in the Jeep, and it had come into full blossom later as he'd watched her making coffee. She had been concentrating on her task and he'd been able to drink in her beauty. He'd never been affected this way before, and knew it was much more than her physical attractiveness. In the short time he had known her, Tegan had inadvertently touched a place in him he had thought permanently calloused over.

The drive from Johnson City to Marble Falls wasn't much more than thirty minutes, but the time seemed to paradoxically fly by as his thoughts centered on Tegan and to crawl at a snail's pace when he faced his anxiety.

Following the directions, he soon pulled into the driveway of a tiny frame house that needed more than a fresh coat of paint to be appealing again. The flower bed that should have been turned under to await next spring's bounty was instead a mass of brown, tangled weeds. The yard had not been edged after last summer's haphazard mowing, and a hanging basket with no occupant swayed dejectedly from a nail stuck into the awning. Steve glanced at the aging Bronco in front of him and thought it might be Billy's, but there was probably more than one rusting yellow Bronco in Marble Falls.

Even though he knew he was stalling, he took some deep breaths before he got out and headed for the front porch. A poorly carved jack-o'-lantern sat on the edge of the concrete, and Steve wondered if any costumed visitors would be by tonight. A sudden burst of laughter from a television diverted his attention, even through the shut door, so Steve knocked loudly. When no response was forthcoming, he tried again, banging with his fist this time.

The door opened with a quick jerk and the look on Billy's face went through several rapid changes. Anger became surprise, then fear, then a sad resignation. Before a word was said, and regardless of Billy's side of the story, Steve already knew the truth.

"It's been a while, Billy."

At Billy's gesture to enter, Steve pulled his Stetson off and stepped inside the cramped house. He noted with detached interest that a feminine hand had tried to make the place a little more comfortable. The curtains were white and frilly, the furniture dusted and polished, and the floors clean. But nothing could hide the fraying edges on the rag rug, or Billy's obviously favorite place—the end of the dilapidated couch.

Billy sat down in the hollow that seemed to have been formed especially for him and waved Steve to a matching and equally threadbare rocker. Billy braced his elbows on his knees and locked his hands together, not meeting Steve's eyes.

"So, how'd you find me?"

"Kenneth Faulkner."

"Oh. I guess you know everything then."

"No, but a fair amount. What happened, Billy?"

"About my place or yours?"

"Both, but start with mine."

Billy picked up a beer bottle from the end table closest at hand, but grimaced when he noted it was empty. "Can I get you one?"

Steve's jaw clenched before he controlled his reaction. "No."

Billy's shoulders pulled back defensively, whether from the coldness in the answer he'd received or from his own discomfort, Steve couldn't tell.

"Well, I need one. I'll be right back."

The trip through the area that served both as living room and dining area couldn't be used as an excuse for much delay, but Billy managed to drag it out enough to cause Steve's jaw to clench again.

Eventually the top was popped off the bottle and Billy returned to the couch.

"So, how's the neck? Are they letting you fly again yet?"

"Not jets. That's why I came home. I'm thinking about getting out."

"Nah! Not you! You're true-blue Navy all the way. You won't retire until you're an admiral."

Steve nailed Billy with a glance. "I'm not here to talk about my military career."

Billy looked off to the left of Steve's shoulder. "I guess not." He heaved a sigh. "I don't know where to start."

"Why don't you start with why you didn't pay the taxes? Or start with why you didn't tell me when things got shaky. You pick."

Billy scraped at the label on his bottle with a thumbnail that needed to see a good nailbrush. "At first, I didn't call you 'cause I thought I'd get everything worked out. Even after the taxes went delinquent, I didn't think it was any big deal because they don't foreclose right away. I know this U.S. marshal who took down some property in Lakeway from a drug dealer, and the taxes on that lot were almost five years old! I was sure I had time to make it come through."

"The problem is, a lady put in a bid on the property so the county had no reason to let it slide," Steve said.

"I know that. Now, anyway. Toward the end, when the IRS was breathing down my neck, I . . . ah, hell, Steve, I know I screwed up. But I just kept putting the letters and stuff away, thinking I'd get to it before things went bad. I had my own worries about the homestead, so I put it out of my mind."

"How did you get around notices being mailed to me? Why wasn't I served with papers?"

Billy's cheeks flushed red. "I used that power of attorney you gave me after Daddy died. It let me sign for the citation on your behalf."

Steve was genuinely surprised. "I don't remember that being in there. Then again, I don't guess I ever imagined anything like this happening."

Rubbing his eyes with weary fingers, Steve let the silence expand. Finally he looked at his cousin again. "Why, Billy? Why didn't you just call me?"

"Man, the trouble in the Middle East was heating up when all this started, and then you got injured. After that, I knew you had too much on your mind with your rehab and stuff. I didn't want to add to your troubles."

Steve forced himself to unclench his fingers and stop crushing his hat. "All this time, Billy. All these years, you never told me. Do you know how I found out?"

Billy shook his head.

"I showed up at the house a few days ago and found a woman living in it. I don't want to admit just exactly what

I accused her of, but basically I called her a liar to her face when she told me the place was hers."

Billy hung his head a moment before a defiant shrug came back into his shoulders. "I've already said I screwed up. But why didn't you come home and check things out? Maybe things wouldn't have worked out this way if you'd have taken care of your own business."

Steve's head jerked back. "Just a minute. I admit I should have been more insistent when I talked with you about the receipts, and maybe I should have come home to check up on you, but it's not my fault you couldn't keep your fingers off the dice."

"Horses."

"Whatever! I just keep coming back to the fact that you didn't call me. I would have helped you, Billy. You're family."

It was Billy's turn to recoil. "I didn't need your damn charity. And if I'd have had just a little more time, I would've made good. It wasn't fair. They didn't give me a chance."

"I don't need excuses, Billy. I simply wanted the truth." He stood and replaced his hat with slow deliberateness. "Now that I've got it, I'll be going."

Billy hurried to stand also, putting the bottle down beside the others on the end table. "Steve...I'm—" He lifted his hands in a futile gesture. "I'm real sorry. Listen, though, I'm going to make it up to you. A buddy of mine wants to go into business and when I get some cash together, you're the first one on my list to pay. I promise."

Steve closed his eyes and pinched the bridge of his nose. "Sure, Billy. Whatever."

"If you do decide to get out, let me know where you move to."

Steve nodded without looking behind him as he reached the door. "Yeah. 'Bye, Billy."

"Take care, man."

Stepping out onto the porch, Steve turned his back to the warm wind that blew against him. He stood there a moment, gazing at the neighbor's porch with unseeing eyes.

Well, now what?

When he climbed into the Jeep once again, he felt as though his legs weighed a thousand pounds. Back out on the highway, he let his mind coast. It had been one hell of a day.

When he hit Johnson City, the sign caught his eye. The town boasted around one thousand people, all of whom were tied to the city by one of three things: family, being in the county seat, or land. All in all, it wasn't exactly a thriving metropolis, and being the county seat was probably all that kept it alive.

He'd been lucky. He'd made it out of the small town, needing more for his life. Oh, he held no scorn for those who flourished in that atmosphere, he just wasn't one of them. He'd hated everyone knowing him and his business, the town-wide expectation for him to succeed not only because he was a star athlete in high school, but because he was Randall Williams's grandson. And yet, through it all, had been the subtle warning for him not to be too successful or he would make others uncomfortable.

But, despite it all, he'd always known where home was, always known where his roots were, always had that place that waited patiently for him to return, beckoning him like a siren's call that promised peace.

And he'd lost it all.

Lost it because he'd been too busy with the Navy, with his career, with the sky. Too busy running away from intimate relationships that were doomed because he wasn't willing to share himself with anyone or anything but his jet. Too busy, too cocky, believing that life wouldn't dare throw him a curve. Too sure that the world revolved around him.

Billy was right, even if it was a whine—it wasn't fair. But then, folks who believed life was fair needed to put down the fairy-tale book. No, it wasn't fair that Billy had a gambling problem, and was working on an alcohol one, as well. Steve snorted. It wasn't fair that he had lost his land because he hadn't been paying attention, either.

His only option, now, looked like convincing a judge and/or jury that he didn't deserve to have his home taken away from him. No matter how corny it sounded, he'd given his all for his country, and his battle back to health was a significant reason for his inattention here at home. He shouldn't have to lose his land as well as his career.

What he needed to do was return to the base and talk to one of the staff attorneys in the Judge Advocate General's office. He appreciated Retta's suggestion about Judge Ohlman, but the JAG would know more of the ins-and-outs of how being in the military affected his situation.

It was still early afternoon when he pulled into the yard. Funny, it felt like he'd been gone a hundred years. He glanced at the house and winced. What should he tell her? The truth about Billy, certainly, but how honest should he be about his plans? Maybe his best bet would be not to say much at all.

Why couldn't he get a lock on this situation? He should devise a logical course of action, review for accuracy, and implement. The problem was, he wasn't operating with Tegan out of the logical, systematical side of his brain. He was operating with her out of the adventurous, go-for-it side. The side that liked to push a plane to the edge of the envelope. To take the risk, feel the thrill. Even though he *should* operate solely out of the first.

Yet in equal measure he was feeling the primal flight-or-fight response to a challenge over his territory. Since running wasn't in his nature, that left the confrontation. He could hardly expect her to understand. Despite the current rift between her and her family, she didn't know what it was like to be an orphan, to be utterly alone in the world, and to realize what an important part this land played in his life. Even if her parents' expectations of her were a little skewed, they still loved her, and it was merely pride that kept her distant. She couldn't know how much this little stone house

and these few acres symbolized security to him, how much
it mattered that he had a place to call home.

He didn't need a psychologist to explain to him why the
Navy had drawn him. The sense of order and discipline had
appealed to a young man who needed to have rules in his
world, where things happened in a logical progression,
where cause and effect were predictable. And he was self-
aware enough to know that the Navy was a surrogate family to him.

And, damn it, he couldn't lose it all in one fell swoop.

But with that thought came his realization that he had to
leave. He was going to fight for his land, and he couldn't,
in good conscience, stay there any longer now that he'd
made up his mind.

With a resigned sigh, he headed for the house.

Desperate to keep occupied, Tegan spent the time while
Steve was away working in the hayloft. She had both ends
of the barn open to every drop of sunshine and every breath
of warm wind.

The weatherman had been right, for once, and the afternoon had rapidly warmed into the seventies. After a week
of near freezing temperatures, combined with wind and
rain, it was a welcome, if amusing respite.

She heard the Jeep pull into the yard as she worked, but
made no move to step outside. She didn't want to see him
yet, to hear his decision, so she kept at her tasks. She'd go
inside later, when she'd worked up her courage.

She hated being subject to his choices, but like it or not,
that was how things stood. Ada's helpful gossip had answered the question of whether or not the tax payments had
been misapplied. So now he held all the cards—in the sense
that he could either walk away and leave her with the land,
or he could fight her for it in court.

If he chose to fight, he would get the fight of his life. Reminding herself of her original arguments, she repeated
them like mantras. This was her land. She had not only paid

money for it, she had put her soul into it. She had worked long and hard for her independence—her financial, emotional, and spiritual independence—and those goals were symbolized in this land. She would let no one take them away from her.

Her call to Enrique earlier had reminded her that she had friends, people who loved her and cared about her, so her worry wasn't about isolation or disconnection. In fact, the exact opposite was true. In following her dreams she had awakened a desire for intimacy in her life and her relationships were more connected than they had ever been. Her experiences with this house and land had been a part of that awakening.

A flash of honesty made her admit that she missed having an intimate relationship with a mate, or rather, she would like to experience one for the first time since she'd never had one before. But if that relationship had to come at the expense of her "self," then she was willing to stay unmated.

A frown marred her forehead. How had her thoughts turned from her vow to fight tooth-and-nail for this land to her desire for a mate? It seemed that if she spent any time at all thinking about Steve, her thoughts strayed in that direction.

That scared her witless.

Steve had literally barged into her life a mere few days ago and yet her thoughts were about intimacy and commitment and...well, good, old-fashioned sex. She hated having to admit that he touched places in her that she thought had healed, only to find them still tender and vulnerable. She thought she had come to terms with her singleness. She thought she had achieved a comfort zone regarding the fact that her choices left her lonely at times.

Steve challenged those ideals. Certainly his effect was inadvertent. It was too frightening to think he might be aware of his power over her.

Shaking her head to force those unwelcome ideas away, she tried for a lighter note. Maybe what was wrong was simple sexual frustration caused by being in close proximity to a handsome, virile man in an emotionally charged atmosphere, and maybe if she just went to bed with him, all this nonsense would go away.

Even before that musing had fully formed, she hid her face in her hands. It was time to get a grip. There was no reasonable explanation for her bizarre contemplations.

Not that the mental picture of Steve naked was bizarre. It was quite evocative, actually. Long, muscular legs, tight buttocks, slim hips—

Stop it, stop it, *stop it!*

Without question, her next move had to be to ask Steve to leave. Regardless of whether he had made a decision or not, she couldn't bear this tension anymore.

As time ticked by, she staunchly refused to go to the other end of the barn and look toward the house. She'd heard his Jeep pull in, and that would be too much like checking on him. But she couldn't help wondering what he was doing, or why he hadn't come looking for her.

Despite her inner turmoil, a glance down made her smile. From her vantage point, she could see the horses grazing contentedly in the near pasture, and when she looked back inside, Good For Nothing was busy fighting dust motes. Tegan leaned on her broom and watched the silly cat crouch and then pounce on a stray piece of hay that had just floated down.

She whipped her head around to the ladder when she heard a low, masculine chuckle.

"I'm glad to know you're safe with that attack cat to guard you."

She thought his smile seemed a bit strained, but still her heart tripped faster as she watched him climb the rest of the way into the loft.

Once she got a full look at his face, she knew.

"You're leaving, aren't you?" she asked, keeping her growing fear from her voice.

He nodded. "It's time." Steve pulled his gaze from hers and glanced around the barn. "Looks like you've been working hard," he said as he bent to scoop Good For Nothing into his arms and tickle under the contented feline's chin. Soon a rumbling purr could be heard halfway across the barn.

Tegan felt the oddest tug in her chest. She quickly dismissed the question of whether or not she would purr if he stroked her like that.

Clearing her throat, she said, "I couldn't sit still so I thought I'd get some work done. Little did I know you'd already finished most of it." She indicated the hayloft, which had been cleared of wet hay after the rainstorm.

His shrug was negligent. "It wasn't that much work, really. You lost one whole bale and I used the dry parts of the couple of others the last time I cleaned the stalls. You were lucky."

Next thing she knew, at a time like this, they'd be talking about the weather!

"Looks like we're in for a couple of days of sunshine." Tegan glanced around her, wondering who said that. Then her eyes grew horrified when she realized it was her own voice.

He managed a chuckle, and tried to smile. Tegan felt the muscles in her neck growing tighter.

Steve glanced at the cat's dreamy expression. "Well, that takes care of the weather. How many safe topics do we have left?"

Tegan sat down on a bale of hay and rested the broom against the wall. Plucking a straw, she twirled it between her fingers. "Let's see, we know we're not supposed to talk about politics, money, sex, or religion....we've exhausted the weather. It's Halloween so I guess we could talk about ghosts and goblins, or maybe what the farmers should plant come spring."

"Hmm, how exciting. I like the ones we're not supposed to talk about better."

"It seems you and I have been doing a lot of things we're not supposed to."

She could tell Steve was stopped short by her statement. His eyes widened as he looked at her intently. He set a disappointed Good For Nothing down and the cat moved off unnoticed.

"Would you care to elaborate on that?"

She could feel the heat flushing her cheeks. "I feel as though I should hate you, or I should have called the sheriff and had you hauled away, or I should have . . . but that's all irrelevant. I didn't do any of the things I *should* have. Instead, I've been cooped up inside an 800-square-foot house with you. I've let you see me at my worst. You have the power to cause me a whole lot of grief.... We both know you're about to leave, and still I sit here, talking to you as casually as if we've been friends for years. I can't get a handle on it."

"I don't want to hurt you, Tegan."

"I don't know that you'll be able to stop it from happening. Unless you're willing to walk away from this situation and never look back, the odds are extremely high that we're going to be locked in combat soon."

His silence was more eloquent than words. At least, she told herself, he didn't offer platitudes or lies.

"I guess I just meant that we probably should only be communicating through our respective attorneys and yet we've . . ." She flushed again. "Oh, I don't know. I feel like we've—"

"Grown fond of each other?"

"If not fond, at least we're concerned about how . . . this is going to affect the other person."

Steve nodded slowly and moved to sit near her on an adjacent bale.

It was time to change the subject slightly. "Do you want to tell me what happened with Billy?" she asked softly.

Running his fingers through his hair in a gesture Tegan had already grown fond of, Steve paused.

"There's not much to say, really. Billy gambled away not only his inheritance, but mine, as well. The clerks didn't make a mistake. I did."

The self-recrimination she heard in his voice touched her. She'd done her fair share of "I should have's" and knew the pain they brought. She hesitated, then put a comforting hand on his arm. A shock cascaded up her arm as soon as she felt the heat of him.

And she knew she'd made a serious mistake.

Nine

Pinned by his eyes, Tegan was lost in the dark brown depths. Her world became focused, narrowed to only the inches between them.

She watched emotions run like quicksilver beneath his eyes, but she was adrift in the sea of her own sensations, unable to capture any of them. She wanted to reach for him, hold him, and make everything go away except the desire. But she was paralyzed.

His rich, dark scent, warmed by the sunlight streaming against his face, came to her. It filled her until she felt weak, dizzy.

She was breathless.

The voice of reason pleaded with her to take her hand away, to move back, to put space between them. The voice went unheeded.

Something urgent, something undeniable, had flared to life from that simple touch. Her last rational thought as Steve moved closer was an acknowledgment that she had to know the taste of him one last time. Maybe she needed to believe she could stop at a kiss, one last touch.

She was wrong.

As soon as his lips moved against hers, she was lost.

No last voice of wisdom could be heard over the rushing of blood in her ears. As Steve dragged her against him, she only knew the fevered urgency of his mouth, his tongue, his hands, the whisper of his breath against her neck.

He whisked away her bandanna and plunged his fingers into her hair, pulling her head back to expose her throat. As he sucked against the pulsing vein, she quaked in his arms.

She grabbed at his chest for balance. Her fingers seemed driven by their own need, and worked at the buttons of his shirt ineptly. With a moan, Steve melded his mouth to hers once more and moved her hands away to rip his shirt open, oblivious to the buttons that flew in all directions. She pushed the shirt from his shoulders. He shrugged out of the confines of the fabric, tossing it behind her on the hay, and reached for her again as though he were starving.

She was on fire.

Everywhere his fingers grazed, every inch of skin his tongue traced, every nip and erotic bite from his strong teeth had her senses pulsing at a fever pitch. When he moved to take the weight of her breast in his palm, she felt a moan start low in her throat.

Desire, blinding and powerful, grew as it swept through her. Never had she experienced a craving this inexorable. She was barely aware that he had removed the last barriers of cloth between them, even though she responded to his demands. It wasn't until his lips captured the tip of one heavy, aching breast, that she received her reward. And even the breath of wind on her now naked skin was almost too potent to bear.

Arching over his arm, she drove her fingers through his hair, pulling him closer. She gulped for air. The heat from his mouth made her melt. The caress of his fingers as one hand splayed across her back made her ache for him to touch her more. Everywhere. Now.

As he laid her down, she clutched at him, opening for him in an urgent, primal invitation. She welcomed the weight of his body against her, holding her breath in anticipation as she felt him pause. Just when she thought she would scream, he moved, sliding slowly, sweetly, to fill her. She closed her eyes to savor every second, every sensation.

He wrapped his arms around her, crushing her breasts into his chest as he began to move. His mouth was against her throat, his breath a hoarse rasp in her ear.

Raking her nails down his back, she stroked his hips and thighs with hands that urged him deeper. The soft whimpers from her throat spurred him on in the dance of passion.

She wanted to protest when he released her, but the sound turned to a gasp as his fingers found her secret place, that aching center crying for fulfillment. As his body moved, as his fingers demanded, as his mouth caressed, she felt the sensations building inside her, taking her to a place so perfect she struggled to reach it.

Then, blindingly, torrentially, it came. A release so complete she thought she would surely faint. She grabbed on to consciousness and forced her eyes open to watch as he flung his head back, squeezed his eyes closed, and experienced the same breathlessly perfect moment.

He dropped his head onto her shoulder and she stroked the sweat-soaked ends of his hair, trailing her caress from his neck to rest her hands on his trembling arms.

Soon, too soon, she felt her spirit, which had soared so high, float back to join her body. She was aware again of the rhythm of her pulse, of the barn around her. And just as she could feel the silken heat of his skin, she could feel the rough pricks of hay under her shoulders.

Steve raised his head and looked down at her. She forced herself to meet his eyes but she couldn't sustain the contact. She saw questions she wasn't willing to articulate yet, much less answer.

Their parting had none of the frantic, yet somehow graceful moments of their joining. She struggled to sit up, ashamed of her inelegance, and tried to cover her chagrin by looking for her clothes. More than her next breath, she needed to get covered.

The silence around them seemed too loud, yet no words came to her to fill it, to change it from oppressive to tolerable.

The sound of a diesel engine pulling into the yard frightened Tegan so badly she slipped off the bale, landing with a ignoble thump on the floor. It was the final straw to an intolerable moment. Heaving herself from the floor, she raced for the end of the loft, peeking around the edge of the open door.

"Oh, my God! It's Enrique and Angelica."

She stood there, unable to move, until the realization hit her that she was still stark naked, except for the shirt she held clutched against her. She was grateful she didn't have to look at Steve as they raced to dress.

"We'll have an extra minute or two while they go to the house." She swore under her breath as her shaking fingers refused to work the buttons on her blouse.

When Steve gently pushed her hands away, Tegan closed her eyes. She wanted to scream at him to leave her alone, but she let him finish the task because of the urgency of the moment. It was all she could do to stand still.

The instant the last button was in place, she backed away to yank on her underwear and jeans. As she stuffed her feet into her shoes, she chanced a glance at Steve and felt a sudden urge to kick him. He was dressed, sitting on a bale of hay, and combing his hair as if it was the most natural thing in the world to do. He had hooked the one still-intact button and then tucked in his shirt. That the rest of the buttons were gone was obvious, but he wore it as though this were his usual attire.

"How can you be so calm?" she snapped, angry at herself for the mildly hysterical note in her voice. She forgave herself in the next instant. How else was she supposed to feel?

Steve handed her his comb and hiked an eyebrow. "What makes you think I'm calm?"

"You're certainly acting like it!" Tegan yanked the tangles and hay from her hair and searched for her bandanna. Her fingers were shaking again as she used the red fabric to tie the barely manageable mass into a ponytail.

"Tegan? Are you in here?" Enrique's deep voice boomed through the barn.

She ran a quick check of her clothes before turning toward the ladder. "Up here, Enrique."

"Where have you been? Didn't you hear—"

Enrique stepped onto the loft and stopped when he saw Steve. Enrique's gaze shifted to her, and Tegan wanted to die. She felt her face heat. By the look on Enrique's face, she knew that he knew. And even if he hadn't figured it out, she'd given it away by blushing.

Enrique's face suffused with anger. He took a step closer and addressed Steve. "So what are you trying to do? Romance the place out from under her?"

"Enrique!" Tegan stared at her friend, appalled. She grabbed his arm with trembling fingers. "Please, stop. I don't...want a scene."

Enrique stared at her. "What has he done to you? Has he hurt you?"

"No, I'm...okay. Please...can we just go to the house?"

"Enrique? Tegan?" A soft, feminine voice called up the ladder. "Are you up there?"

Tegan closed her eyes, not sure she could take much more. She was ashamed to feel herself sway on her feet.

Steve put a steadying hand under her arm. She despised the weakness but knew she'd be foolish to deny his support. With a curt nod, she thanked him. With a severe glance, she warned Enrique to back off.

When she nodded again, Steve went down the ladder first and watched her carefully as she descended. Angelica's welcoming smile as she moved forward to hug Tegan turned confused. When she saw her brother's scowl, Angelica's expression turned wary.

After several deep breaths, Tegan felt her equilibrium somewhat restored. She turned on her heel and headed for the house, not sure she cared if any of the rest of the crowd followed or not. Once inside, she busied herself making coffee, more for something to keep her hands busy than out of a desire to play hostess. She heard Steve excuse himself and head through the living room. The scraping noises behind her led her to believe Enrique and Angelica had taken seats at the kitchen table.

There was only so much stalling filling a coffeepot could buy. Desperate for a moment alone, she ran upstairs and locked herself in the bathroom to bathe her face in cool water. The eyes that stared back at her as she recombed her hair and pulled it back looked like they belonged to someone else. The blue orbs reflected were empty, hollow. Lost.

She heard faint traces of Steve still in his bedroom and decided that she needed to avoid running into him at all costs. Caught between the choice of facing Steve or facing her friends, she chose Enrique and Angelica and hurried back to the kitchen.

Enrique's expression was still angry, his lips tightened judgmentally. Angelica was curious, and concerned.

"What the hell was that all about?" Enrique demanded.

Tegan searched for an explanation until something inside her snapped. A fortifying, steadying indignation surged through her.

"None of your damned business."

Enrique had the sense to look chagrined. "I'm just trying to take care of you."

"I don't need you, or anyone else to take care of me. No matter how well-intentioned, you're sticking your nose where it doesn't belong."

A sound at the swinging doors made all three heads turn toward the living room. Steve stood just inside the kitchen in a fresh shirt, with a hastily packed duffel bag hefted over his shoulder. Tegan wondered if he had heard her words, but decided it didn't matter.

Steve met her eyes directly, his face a solemn but polite mask.

"Is there... can I... do anything to help?" she asked.

"I'll take a thermos of that coffee, if it's no trouble."

"None at all." She struggled for the same nonchalant expression that seemed to come so easily to Steve. For all that he revealed, she could have been a waitress at Ada's taking his order.

With Tegan, Enrique and Angelica trying desperately not to be obvious about their watching, Steve accomplished the repacking of his Jeep in about the same time he'd unpacked it. When she thought that a thunderstorm had hurried him in before but an emotional one hurried him out now, Tegan almost laughed.

Almost.

The minutes had dragged by until she thought her nerves would snap. Finally, with the last of his gear loaded, Steve stepped into the kitchen, his hat in his hand.

"I'll be taking off."

Tegan brought the thermos to him. She could hardly believe it possible, but she felt even more awkward than moments before.

Steve took the coffee, absurdly careful not to brush her fingers.

"Could you... would you walk with me for a minute?"

Tegan nodded. When she heard a chair scrape the floor, she cast a quick glare over her shoulder. Enrique reseated himself with a small huff.

The screen banged shut behind her and Tegan noted absently that the afternoon sunlight was rapidly fading into dusk. She thrust her fingers into her front pockets and hunched her shoulders forward. The air had turned cooler.

Following behind, she looked at Steve's posture-perfect back. She supposed this was inevitable, but she still wished it was over and he was gone. Then she planned on going to her room, pulling the covers over her head, and never coming out.

Tegan wondered why she was startled to see the horse trailer hooked up to the Jeep. It wasn't as though he would leave Ghost Dancer behind, but somehow the horse had become a part of her world and she felt a pang of sadness that the beautiful gelding wouldn't be there to nicker a welcome the next time she went in to tend Dream Chaser.

The thought jarred her memory and she looked toward the barn. She should have known. He had closed it up, and she was sure when she went in, everything would be neatly in its place—just empty of the traces of Steve and Ghost Dancer.

Steve opened the door to the Jeep, holding on as he turned toward her. "Tegan, I'm—"

That spine-straightening anger was back. "Don't you dare say you're sorry," she snapped. "You can say anything but that."

A hint of a smile tugged at his mouth. "Good, because I wasn't going to. I was planning to say that I'm stationed at Alvin Calendar Field in New Orleans. I left a note on your desk with some phone numbers if you need me."

"Okay."

When Steve hesitated, Tegan managed a brief smile.

"Tegan, are you...all right?"

Her short laugh contained no humor. "No."

At Steve's startled, worried look, she felt compelled to add, "I will be, though. Don't worry about me."

Steve laughed this time, something between a grunt and a chuckle. "Like that's possible." He jammed his hat on his head. "It's probably best if I get going. I'm not making this any easier on either of us."

"That's true," Tegan agreed with unusual bluntness. It was the only way she could maintain even this semblance of control.

Steve winced but she refused to feel remorse.

"I'll be in touch."

Tegan snorted. "Don't make any promises you don't intend to keep."

A steely coldness returned to his eyes. "I don't lie, Tegan, but you can choose to believe what you like. Look, this isn't the best time to say this, but it's doubtful there'll be another chance. While this is in limbo, if you need anything, anything at all, call me. I know all the folks around here so I can send help your way."

Stiff-necked, she regarded him. "Why can't I seem to make anyone understand that I can take care of myself. I don't need your help."

Steve resumed his expressionless, unreadable mask. "I didn't intend my offer to be an insult."

She closed her eyes for a second and sighed. "I know."

"Goodbye, Tegan."

"Goodbye, Steve."

He got in the Jeep and slammed the door shut. She turned and headed back, flinching when the engine started and the gears ground into place. She sneaked a peek over her shoulder when she reached the house, but he had already made the first turn down the road.

When Tegan reentered the kitchen, Angelica's rapid, heated Spanish directed at Enrique stopped abruptly. Tegan was glad she didn't speak the language, if her friend's face was any indication of the nature of her tirade.

Enrique started to speak, but Tegan held up her hand. "Guys, you know I love you both dearly, but I've got to be alone right now. I'm heading for bed. I don't know how long I'll be there." She rubbed her forehead with shaking fingers. "You've stayed out here enough—you know where everything is. Make yourselves at home, okay?"

Even knowing that her choices were to get to her room quickly or break down in front of her friends, Tegan forced herself to walk slowly through the living room. As she climbed the stairs, she felt the two sets of worried eyes that followed her every step.

She hoped Enrique and Angelica believed her. She cared very much for her friends, and appreciated their concern, but her restraint on a screaming, crying fit was tenuous at best. She had no strength left for the most mundane conversation, much less a heated discussion about whether or not she'd lost her mind. Which she admitted was possible.

She'd lied. She headed for the bathroom instead of her bedroom, and went straight to the shower. With one hand braced against the tile wall, she kept her face in the spray as long as she could hold her breath. Then she bent her head forward and let the hot water pound her neck, her eyes clenched against the rivulets that streamed over her face.

Despite herself, she had glanced around the bathroom as she'd undressed, but Steve had been thorough that morning. There was nothing left behind to remind her of him. Nothing physical, anyway. Just the lingering aroma of his shaving cream and the spicy smell of his cologne. He'd even cleaned the sink of the traces of his shaving.

How thoughtful.

Pushing the snide thought away, she went through the motions of her shower. She realized that she hadn't intended to wash the scent of him off her, but now that it was done she was glad.

The shower, though, could not wash the memories from her mind and she knew those would be there to haunt her forever. For now, the aftermath of the emotional carnage of the day left her weak and so exhausted that she stumbled on her way through her room. Using her dresser to steady herself, she got into a gown, scrubbed her hair one last time with the towel, and crawled under the covers.

For once, thankfully, blessedly, sleep did not elude her.

Ten

Steve let himself into his apartment and threw his duffel bag onto the couch. The last leg of his journey home—after taking Ghost Dancer to the stables—had seemed to take longer than the previous seven hours combined. He'd been grateful, since it was the wee hours of the morning, that he had a friend with a small stable who took care of Ghost Dancer and let him come and go as he pleased. Otherwise, he would never have been able to keep a horse.

At least, he should be grateful. Instead he was tense and frustrated. He alternated between a numb nothingness and reliving every moment he had held Tegan in his arms, buried between the silken heat of her thighs, hearing her moans of passion against his ear—

He shook his head forcefully. He had to stop it. He had to stop thinking about her.

Yet as he glanced around the apartment, the first thing that hit him was how... neutral... it appeared. Everything was beige and brown with a little green tossed in now and then.

There weren't any brilliant splashes of color, any deep, cushiony places, any knickknacks. The only truly personal possession was the framed photograph of his grandparents that sat on the mantel over the fireplace.

He had some plaques and awards, but they were mounted in the second bedroom that served as his office. And he wasn't sure those counted in the comparisons he was making.

All right, he'd admit it. Tegan had made the ranch house her home. It carried her mark in every room. He'd never done that in any of the places he'd lived. He used to think it was part of being military, but the truth was, he'd never wanted to be anything more than transient. It had been easy and convenient to know, in the back of his mind, that the ranch was waiting. It made it simpler to avoid the effort of transforming a residence into a home.

A glance at the clock told him it was almost two o'clock in the morning. He felt every minute of it. All he wanted to do was fall into bed and sleep for a week. Anything to stop his thoughts for a while.

Instead he only slept twelve hours. Just a short reprieve.

Groggy, head throbbing, he stumbled to the bathroom and searched for an aspirin. The face that greeted him in the mirror seemed foreign. Not because he was unshaven and disheveled. That was life every morning. Or afternoon, as the case may be. It was the hollowness in his eyes that he'd never seen.

He'd been tired before. Tired beyond anything imaginable, and still conscious. He'd been in pain that bad and worse.

But he'd never felt this empty. Not even when they'd grounded him, taken away any hope of flying fighters again, when they'd stolen from him the only thing that mattered. Not even then.

Pushing away from the sink, he shoved aside the maudlin thoughts. All he needed to do was to concentrate on the tasks at hand—finish unloading the Jeep, put his things away, laundry, grocery store. . . .

Call the Judge Advocate General's office.

He had plenty of time, he assured himself. And he had a buddy on the JAG's staff so he could get some answers right away just by asking—

A pounding on the door demanded his attention. He yanked on a pair of shorts and answered the impatient summons.

"Hey, Steve! Saw your Jeep and stopped by. I thought you were going to be gone a couple of weeks."

"Hey, Ross. I just got in this morning. Change of plans."

"Something wrong?" Ross asked as he helped himself to a drink from the refrigerator.

"No, just slept too long."

"You look like hell."

Steve was surprised he could chuckle. "Thanks." Then a thought occurred to him. "What are you doing off base at this time of day?"

"I took some annual leave myself."

Something in Ross's voice clued him. "And?"

"I'm moving in with Gina."

Steve eyed him suspiciously. "So why do I get the impression you don't want to be congratulated."

Ross shrugged. "It was one of those ultimatum things and I caved. This was my compromise."

"I take it she's still going for the ring."

After a swig, Ross nodded. "Man, why are women always trying to push you into things you don't want? Or making you feel guilty when you do the things you gotta do? Makes me nuts, man. Say, wanna play some racquetball?"

It was tempting. An easy excuse to avoid doing what he needed to do. And he had every confidence that he'd feel worse than guilty when he did it.

"I thought you were busy moving."

Ross grimaced as he swallowed. "Yeah, I'm supposed to be."

"Thanks, but I don't want to get on Gina's bad side. I'll catch you another time."

Ross straightened and headed toward the door. "Later, man."

Steve echoed the goodbye and went to work. In the next hour, he ate, showered, shaved, dressed, and located the power of attorney.

He sat down as he read the document. But there it was, in black and white. *To represent and act for me in all tax matters in dispute or litigation, in any governmental department, board or court...*

When he'd read every word of every line, he put in a call to the JAG's office. By the time he replaced the receiver, Steve doubted his spirits could get much lower. He traced his pen around the name of the civilian attorney his contact had recommended, nearly tearing a hole in his blotter.

For the next hour, while he finished putting away his things, he went over and over the information he'd been given. From the surface review, it looked as if he would get no help from the military angle. It might have been a great help if not for the power of attorney, but that was a moot point.

He had been advised that he could sue Billy for breach of fiduciary duty, but Steve immediately vetoed that option. He'd never been one to kick a man while he was down, and even if he was so inclined, Billy had no assets.

His only real option was the one he'd known all along. He could file a lawsuit against Blanco County with Tegan as a co-defendant, plead his extenuating circumstances, and hope a jury would see things his way. Since the county had acted in good faith, he'd have a fight on his hands, but his hope lay in getting an extension to file an appeal.

Reluctantly he dialed the attorney's number and made an appointment.

* * *

Tegan pulled her truck under the awning and sat there with her hands on the steering wheel. She glanced at the barn, picturesque against the roiling mass of clouds, and memories flooded her. Slowly she lowered her head to rest it against the back of her hands.

Could it really have been only ten days since Steve had left? Ten days since she'd been reckless—passionately, wildly, madly reckless—in the loft of that barn? Had she really had day after endless day of her thoughts filled with the memory of his taste, his touch, his smell, his voice?

Tegan sat back and let her hands fall into her lap. Sitting here in the truck wasn't going to accomplish anything, but she felt it would be a monumental effort to move.

She was so tired. Bone-weary was an inadequate description. It bothered her that she was much more tired than a mere week of seminars should have made her.

In fact, her utter exhaustion and Angelica's concern were the reasons she had stopped by her doctor's office today on the way home. She had decided it was worth the few dollars to have a simple blood test run. She'd bet she was having some left-over symptoms from the flu.

Deciding she'd unpack her stuff later, Tegan scooped up the mail she'd dumped on the passenger seat and headed inside the house. The messages on her answering machine were all innocuous so she erased the tape and reset it. Plopping herself down on the couch, she started sorting through the pile of letters and advertisements she'd brought in. She stopped short when she saw a heavy parchment envelope from an attorney in Louisiana. Behind it was another bearing Steve's return address, written in bold, neat script.

Her stomach turned sour as she opened his letter. Well, he'd contacted her all right. She had expected a phone call. In fact, she'd jumped every time the phone had rung for the first few days after he was gone.

She'd never dreamed she'd come home from a week of seminars to find these two little bombshells in her waiting stack of mail.

The letter was short, concise, unapologetic—explaining he felt he had made enough mistakes and had to buy himself some time. He was doing so by filing a lawsuit, even though he still wasn't sure what his final decision would be.

He had included an offer to buy the place from her, which she had to admit—if she was being reasonable—was a fair one. He'd then stated she would get a letter from his attorney making an official proposal. If she accepted the offer, he would, of course, immediately dismiss the lawsuit. She didn't even open the letter from the attorney.

Wadding Steve's letter into a ball, she threw it across the room and watched with little satisfaction as it fell short of the fireplace. She had no intention of being reasonable. It didn't matter if he offered her a million dollars, he wasn't going to buy her out.

Anger boiled in her, and under that was a layer of fear. She was angry—at Steve, at herself, at her friend who'd pointed the property out to her, at her parents, at her ex-husband . . . at everybody.

She recognized the anger as a cover, but it was easier to be angry than afraid. And if her fear ran equal with her rage, she was terribly scared. Experience had shown her what a good attorney could do, and just how long cases could be dragged out. The "wear down the other side by waiting" game was actually a pretty good strategy. It would have worked for the Weasel, but her attorney had helped her stand firm. And her reward for enduring the grueling mental contest had been this ranch.

She looked around the room, noting the changes she had made, and the ones still waiting to be accomplished. Every time she thought about it, another decision had to be made. Should she stick with her schedule of renovations or should she wait to see what happened? On the one hand, it would conserve money she might end up needing for attorney's fees. Her cash reserves weren't large enough to make her comfortable. On the other hand, if she didn't keep working on her plans, it would mean he had already won a tactical victory by making her doubt her ownership.

She slapped the table with her palm, but it didn't do much in the way of venting her frustration. She fought the urge to kick something next. Chances were, she'd be in limbo for a long time, and patience was another one of the things she'd lost in the divorce.

Her vow made long ago—that she would never let anyone push her around again—was coming back to haunt her. She was being pushed, all right. Whether she liked it or not.

A weary sigh escaped as she hunched her back and shoulders to relieve the aches.

It had turned bitterly cold again.

Walking into the kitchen, she leaned on the cool tile while she looked out the window over the sink. The sky was as gray as her spirit and the air was damp. Not unusual weather for the middle of November, although there were no guarantees it wouldn't be in the eighties tomorrow. She watched the wind grab and shake the bare branches of the giant pecan tree that stood guard by the barn. Dead leaves danced across the yard in little whirlpools before dispersing. It was the perfect analogy for her mood—brown, drab, listless, but with moments of frenzied activity.

She glanced at the stack of wood waiting to be split and shivered even though she was inside. The wind would cut through her with little effort. Then again, some tough, physical exercise might just be the thing. Despite herself, she smiled. The first few times she'd tried to split her own wood, she'd ended up splitting her sides from laughing so hard. Inept would have been a kind word to use for her prowess then. Now she could run through a whole cord without thinking about it.

It was just another one of those little things, those on-the-surface, inconsequential things, that made this place hers. It was just one of the myriad ways she had grown, adapted.

She had found a new strength, a new skill inside her that she hadn't known was there. It took a certain amount of dexterity to swing an ax, and she was proud of herself.

In minutes she had changed into work clothes, grabbed the receiver unit off the cordless to take with her, and was out the back door.

Set up. Swing. Stack the pieces. Set up. Swing... The rhythm took over, a welcome escape. When she heard a familiar diesel engine come into the yard, she was vaguely disappointed to have her work interrupted.

Wiping her forehead on her sleeve, Tegan turned to find out which of the two Esquivels had come this time. It was Enrique.

"Hey, gorgeous lady." He engulfed her in a hug and kissed her windblown cheek.

"Hello, Enrique. What brings you out? I don't have any strange men here for you to run off with your brooding glances."

He flushed. "I don't brood."

"Yes, you do. So, answer the question." She was still perturbed with her headstrong friend, but her initial resentment had faded.

"Can't I just come out and see you?"

"Yes, but you have several businesses to run. You normally just come and see me on the weekends."

"Since it's Monday, we'll call it a long weekend. Okay?"

Tegan relented. "I guess. Where's Angelica?"

"She said to tell you she's working on a coconut quilt and will come show it to you soon."

Tegan's brow furrowed. "Do you mean a pineapple quilt?"

Enrique rolled his eyes. "Whatever."

Instantly, absurdly, Tegan thought that Steve wouldn't have made that mistake. Or, at the least he would have shown appreciation for the project, not impatience.

And that reminded her to check on the quilts at the restorer's. They were probably ready.

Great! Another decision to make. Would she keep her word and give the quilts to him, or retain them and feel spiteful? Right now, spiteful won.

They had stood chatting for so long her body had cooled off. Tegan shivered as a gust of wind whipped down the collar of her flannel shirt. She had been warm while swinging that ax, but no longer.

"Do you want to come in?" she asked, as she retrieved her jacket and headed for the house.

"Sure. And—"

Tegan heard the phone ring and glanced back at the cordless unit by the woodpile. In the next second, she calculated she was closer to the house and started running. Racing in, she grabbed the receiver off the kitchen wall and said, breathlessly, "I'm here!"

She listened to the nurse's voice and felt the blood drain from her face. "What did you say?" Clutching the wall to stay upright as the nurse repeated herself, Tegan managed to add, "Thank you for calling," before hanging up.

Enrique rushed to her side as she stumbled into a chair and hid her face in her hands.

"Tegan! What's wrong?"

She shook her head, fighting the infuriating urge to cry. This couldn't be happening.

"Tegan, you'd better tell me right now what's the matter."

She lifted her head but couldn't meet his eyes. "Enrique, I'm pregnant."

She saw him recoil as if she'd slapped him.

"What?" he whispered. "I thought you couldn't have children."

"That's what I thought, too. Obviously, I was wrong."

"How? When?"

Amazingly, Tegan felt a mixture of amusement and offense at Enrique's tone. "As to how, the usual way. When? On Halloween."

She almost smiled as she watched Enrique pull his shoulders back as though preparing for a blow. "Who's the father?"

"I think you know the answer to that, too."

"It was that Steve guy, right?"

She nodded.

"What are you going to do?"

She struggled against the hysterical laughter that bubbled up in her throat. "I haven't had a lot of time to think about it yet, Enrique. I don't know."

"Are you going to tell him?"

"I don't know!" She crossed her arms over her chest and mutinously refused to feel guilty for yelling.

"I can't believe this is happening."

"You can't believe it? You're not the one who's pregnant!"

Enrique pinned her with a glance. "No, but I'm the one who wanted to father your children."

He spoke the words so softly they tore right through her heart. Tears welled in her eyes and she struggled to breathe.

"Enrique, I—"

A knock cut her off. Her heart began to race. Could it be Steve? She hurried toward the door. Surely he would have called—

The man at the door wasn't Steve. When she took in the five-pointed star pinned to his chest, her heart fell and her face flushed. How could she have been so stupid?

"Good afternoon, ma'am. Are you Tegan E. McReed?"

Sniffing quickly, she dashed at her eyes. "Yes, I am."

"I need to serve you with this citation."

Tegan reached out automatically as he handed her some folded sheets of white paper.

Tipping his hat again, the deputy backed out of the doorway. "Thank you, ma'am."

She shut the door, stunned, even though she knew she shouldn't be. At least he hadn't told her to have a nice day.

She probably would have slugged him and gotten arrested for assaulting an officer.

She opened the pages and saw the style of the case.

Her stomach threatened to heave.

She'd known this was coming. It shouldn't hurt this much. It shouldn't feel as though someone had stomped on her and then wrapped her lungs in a vise.

"Tegan?"

It was another minute before she could look up at Enrique, hovering near her shoulder.

As if he couldn't bear to see the look in her eyes, he started talking—fast, as though he was trying to get everything out at once. "Tegan, I can't stand to see you like this. Let me take care of you. Marry me. I'll claim the baby is mine. And we can fight this. You can use my lawyer—"

"Enrique, stop!" She wanted to soften the blow, find a diplomatic way of saying it, but the only thing that would come out was the truth. "I can't let you do this."

"But I want to. You're so special to me. Don't you know I lo—"

She put her fingers to his lips. "Please, Enrique, don't say it. It'll only force me to put distance between us, and right now, I need you as my friend."

He smiled weakly, reaching out to stroke the hair back from her face. "You're really something special, you know." His voice dropped to a husky whisper. "I wish it could have been me."

Moving into his arms, she hugged him tightly. Since words failed her, she hoped she conveyed to him just how important he was to her. He kissed her forehead and she closed her eyes. Why couldn't it have been him? It would have made things so much easier.

She hated to admit it, but she'd had a safety net in Enrique. He'd been willing to wait in the wings, just in case she might want him for more than a friend some day, and she'd been willing to let him. But it wasn't fair and it wasn't right. And no matter how scared she was, she had to let him go.

She had to do this on her own, no matter how tempting it was to let him shoulder her burden.

Enrique put his hands on her arms and gently pushed her away. "I'd probably better leave."

"Probably."

He chucked her under the chin. "Will you call me if you need anything?"

Her gesture was something between a shrug and a nod. She couldn't outright lie to him so she sidestepped. "Thanks. For everything."

He pulled on his jacket and walked away. He stopped as he opened the door, turning back to look at her for a long time before closing it behind him.

Tegan leaned against the wall, straining to hear the sound of his engine, until she was sure he was gone.

Then she was alone.

Utterly, completely alone.

Slowly, she slid down the wall and gave in to tears.

Eleven

Steve drained the last of his beer. Beer and fried chicken.
Not exactly the usual Thanksgiving spread.

Stepping out onto the balcony, he squinted at the brilliant blue sky. The weather had turned out gorgeous. He
listened to the radio with half an ear and caught the tail end
of the forecast. The weatherman said the entire south and
southeast would enjoy several more days of warm after-
noons and cold nights before the next front hit.

He wondered what the temperature was in Johnson City.

Shaking his head, he ignored the passing thought and
tried to get lost in the music blaring from his speakers. He
was restless, and knew sitting around in loneliness wasn't the
answer. On autopilot, he put on his running shorts and
headed for the trails. The nearby park was one of the reasons he'd picked this location.

So, what were some of the others? a voice inside his head
asked him. What had drawn him to this place? Nothing
special, was the truthful answer. The basics—reasonable rent, good neighborhood, near enough to the base.

Enough of this already! He'd run the apartment-versus-the-ranch argument around in his head so many times he thought he was going to go nuts. One day he was sure that the homestead meant everything to him, and the next he was ready to call the attorney and tell him to forget the whole thing.

So how did he quiet the voices in his head? One voice made him feel worse than scum for what he was doing to Tegan; the other told him he would be crazy to give up everything without taking time to think things through.

Well, he'd done nothing but. For four weeks now he'd thought about her constantly. He remembered her almost desperate hold on her control. He could see the fear and confusion in her eyes. And the loneliness she tried to conceal.

He could also recall every second, every breath of their lovemaking. He saw, in vivid detail, the honey color of her hair, the lapis blue of her eyes, and her reluctant, stunning smiles. And all he had to do was get a whiff of anything that smelled like peach and he could close his eyes and swear he had her neck against his mouth.

He stumbled on the track. Forcing himself to concentrate, he picked up his rhythm again.

One voice dismissed those memories as hormones. The other tried to tell him he was in lo—

No, he couldn't even think it.

But was the evidence right in front of his eyes? Was he being deliberately obtuse? He'd had four weeks to get over what had happened—four long, frustrating weeks—and yet every day was filled with more of the memory of her, not less.

Not the land, not the lawsuit.

Her.

Wondering if she was okay, if she needed anything.

If she hated him.

He deserved it if she did. A thousand times he'd wanted to pick up the phone and call her. And each time he hadn't. It wouldn't be fair to do that to her until he had made up his mind.

And when he wasn't thinking about her, he was thinking about getting out of the service. Sometime the thought of resigning his commission sounded utterly absurd. At others, he knew that the Navy was no longer home. It was just a job now. He had lost that sense of completeness that had accompanied his career. He knew, now, that there was more to life than achieving his next rank. New needs had been awakened in him these past few weeks, needs he hadn't had any idea existed. And they were needs that would not be denied.

He needed someone to talk to. Someone he could confide in and receive some feedback from that wasn't biased. He smiled when he realized who he wanted to go see. Okay, so his choice wasn't exactly unbiased, but at least Admiral Grissom was someone he trusted.

A little over an hour later, Steve found himself back at his apartment with his mind made up. The admiral had grilled him unmercifully, but in the end, had agreed to facilitate the paperwork for Steve resigning his commission.

Grabbing his duffel bag, Steve started packing. If he worked quickly, he could get Ghost Dancer and be back at the ranch by ten or eleven that evening.

He was going back to claim what was his.

Tegan poked dejectedly at her turkey pot pie and grimaced. Hardly a Thanksgiving feast, but it was fast and didn't require any thought or preparation.

Tegan decided she couldn't take much more emotional turmoil in her life. It seemed all she'd done for the past four weeks was think, debate and ponder. And cry.

Before all this, she probably could have counted on one hand the number of times she'd shed tears. Since the lawsuit and the pregnancy, that theory no longer held true. She could now more easily count the times she didn't cry.

Oh, well, since she seemed to have been given one stroke of good luck by avoiding morning sickness, she should hardly begrudge her system a few tears.

It had been the swings from sadness to anger that had been the most wrenching, she found. The anger had eventually dissipated, leaving her feeling lost and horribly alone. She'd then done something she hadn't thought about in a long time. She'd started a new journal. Writing out the emotional maelstrom had helped her focus again, decide what she wanted. The process had also been intensified by her isolation, her inability to use a busy social life to keep her from dealing with her thoughts. It had taken forever, but she'd gained some sympathy for Steve, even though she reaffirmed her vow to fight for the property.

Then she'd remember the baby and would start wondering what in heaven's name she was going to do. A new life was coming into this world and it would be completely dependent on her. She'd just barely reached the stage where she could take care of herself. How could she care for a child? Babies required so much love. Could she do it? Could she provide all that a child needed? She wanted to be so much more than just a mother, could she be a mom?

Her own mother's call earlier, ostensibly to invite her to come home for Thanksgiving dinner, had only increased her dilemma. Part of her wanted to confide in her mother, but Tegan knew better than to tell Diedre about the baby. The choice had been quickly taken out of her hands when the call had degenerated into an argument about her life-style. Tegan had felt inclined to call her mother shallow and materialistic, to which Diedre had replied that Tegan was obviously following in close footsteps for the ranch obviously was as much a gem to her as any of Diedre's diamonds were to herself.

The truth had stung more than Tegan cared to admit.

After some thought Tegan felt she could honestly say her mother was wrong. Yes, Tegan was proud of her home and was not ashamed of the quality of her possessions. But what her mother obviously did not see, did not understand, was that Tegan's pride came from the accomplishment of her goals, not the accumulation of things. The house, the ranch, were just symbols. It wasn't the land itself, it was—

Tegan slowly straightened her posture.

It wasn't the land itself that was important. It was the growth she'd achieved. She loved this house, this ranch, but the fact was that it shouldn't matter where she lived. The integral parts of herself, her achievements, would move with her wherever she went. And even though part of this ranch now belonged to the baby, she knew she would always be able to provide well for her child.

Maybe the seemingly unending days of mental examination hadn't been just to torture her. Maybe it had been a part of a plan to soften her, make her more accepting to an alternative that had been unpalatable in the beginning.

She'd learned from this experience, gained valuable insight into herself. While it would be hard to leave—if she chose to or had to—she knew now, in a deep and comforting way, that she wouldn't be devastated.

The longer she sat there, the more quickly the thoughts flowed through her mind. It seemed natural to conclude that if she accepted this ranch as just a part of her journey, and not the culmination of it, then she could face letting Steve have what he so passionately believed was his. She could quit arguing with herself over whether or not she was legally right and morally wrong.

Needing a breather, she threw her cold dinner in the trash. Pouring herself a glass of milk, she went outside to watch the sunset only to find the cold front, which wasn't supposed to hit for another three days, was moving through. Shivering in the biting wind, she went back inside and built a fire instead.

Kicking off her shoes, she grabbed a lap quilt and snuggled into the cushions to enjoy the warmth of the flames bathing her face. As she watched, mesmerized by the light, her mind strayed. It took no effort to imagine the light on Steve's face as he'd made love to her, feel where the sun had warmed his hair as she ran her fingers through the silky strands. His lips and tongue had set her skin ablaze hotter than the logs in the fireplace and she had felt just as consumed.

In a moment of honesty she admitted that he was never far from her thoughts. Sometimes she was angry with him, sometimes she ached for him, sometimes she sympathized with him. But always, he was there. Often the memories were so real she felt she could close her eyes and reach out, and her fingers would again feel the heat of his skin.

She pulled herself back, forcing herself to return to her original thoughts. The questions of right and wrong didn't matter anymore because her mother, even though she didn't know it, had given her a gift. And in return, she could give Steve a gift. Well, maybe not *give* him a gift. She would at least think about accepting his offer to buy the property and use the money to start again.

What she would give him, with no strings attached, were the nine beautiful quilts that she'd paid a fortune to have restored. She would feel torn to give those back, but they truly hadn't been hers from the moment she'd learned their history. They were Steve's legacy.

Which left only the huge hurdle of whether or not to tell him about the baby. If she let him have the land and moved away soon, he'd never know.

She buried her face in her hands. Oh, God! Another moral dilemma! Was it her right to keep knowledge of the baby from him? She didn't intend to ask him for anything. She didn't need his name or his money.

The insistent voice was back: did he or did he not have the right to know about the baby?

If they had any chance at all for a future together, of course she would tell him about the baby. But the fact was, for all that she felt as though she'd known Steve forever, the reality remained that they were nearly strangers. They had nothing in common to build a relationship upon. Incredible sex could not be the foundation of a lasting union.

And since there was no hope of them ever being partners, there was no need to burden him with a child he didn't want, right? She might not know much about the military, but she doubted Steve was looking for a wife. No guy that good-looking, that successful, that alluring, remained single this long unless he was determined to stay that way. Regardless of his military status, she was absolutely sure that Steve had no lack of ready, willing and available women to marry if he'd ever so desired. She was no psychologist, but she'd bet a nickel he had no intention of being pinned down. Not to the earth, not to a woman, and that meant, ergo, not to a baby.

On top of all that, she had to add another aspect of Steve's military background. He was an officer, authoritarian by nature, used to having his wishes obeyed instantly and without question. She couldn't do that. She wouldn't do that. He might be Mr. Nice Guy for a while, but when the rosy haze of a new romance wore off, she had to believe he would revert to his true nature and she could never be a military wife.

Her mental wrangling left her even more defiant than before. Didn't she have the right to control her own destiny? Didn't she have the right, for once in her life, to make a decision based solely on what was right for her? How did one indiscreet moment give him the right to interfere in her life forever?

By God, she wasn't about to give up control of her destiny. Even if he was the greatest guy in the world, that didn't obligate her to alter forever the path of her future for his sake. For the first time in her life, she was autonomous, obligated only to herself. She didn't have a boss to answer to, she didn't have to answer to her parents, and she didn't have to answer to a husband any more. She wasn't about to start doing so again. Ever.

This baby was *hers*, damn it. For so many years now, she'd wanted a child of her own. More than anything, she'd wanted to hold a precious little life in her arms and know that indescribable joy as she watched her son or daughter sleep against her breast. Now, despite a bizarre set of circumstances, that dream was going to come true and she wasn't going to let anything or anyone get in her way.

But what about the child's rights? Didn't the child have the right to know about his or her father? To know a man who was proud and strong. Dedicated. Honorable.

Honorable? The man who'd filed a lawsuit against her?

Yes. The answer came back clearly. He had done the only thing he could, under the circumstances, and he hadn't done it maliciously.

Great. Now she was no closer to a solution than before. The issue of the land was out of the way, only to leave her with a much bigger, much more consequential decision.

Tegan felt her eyelids getting heavy and with a thankful sigh, slipped into the escape of sleep.

Steve smiled as he hit the edge of Johnson City. Not even the sleet tapping on his windshield, which wasn't supposed to hit for three more days, could dampen his mood.

Against all rationality, all logic, he loved her. Why else would he be breaking the speed limit on Thanksgiving Day to drive across Louisiana and half of Texas to return to a woman who would probably slam the door in his face?

He hadn't even taken the time to close down his apartment. He'd left a message on a buddy's machine telling him to come clean out the beer and junk food from the refrigerator. Everything else could wait to be hauled to the ranch another day.

On his way out of town he'd stopped by the lawyer's office to slip an envelope under the door. His letter instructed that the lawsuit be dismissed and an agreement drawn up that he relinquished all right to the property. He'd ended by asking the attorney to send the papers to the ranch after the judge had signed the order.

It was all he could do to keep his speed at a safe level. The closer he got to home, the more anxious he became.

Natural questions came to mind. What would she think? Would she throw him out on his ear? Should he have called first?

The last question was easy to answer. It might not be the most gentlemanly thing to do, but he wasn't going to take any chances. He felt his odds were better just showing up.

Suddenly his hands tightened on the steering wheel. What if she wasn't home? In all his planning, in all the hours on the road, it had never occurred to him that she might not be there. It was Thanksgiving, after all.

Well, if she wasn't, he'd backtrack to the nearest hotel and wait until she returned.

He regretted that this would shock her. He only hoped he didn't scare her. Part of him had urged him to stay in New Orleans until the order had come back from the judge, but he couldn't face waiting that long. He'd made enough mistakes already. He wasn't going to add another one.

He felt sure his reception would be chilly, to say the least, but he had every intention of wooing her and winning her. It wouldn't be easy, but it would be worth it.

He was prepared for a siege. He would wear down her defenses until she fell in love with him.

He refused to even consider that he might fail.

Pulling into the yard, he noticed the house was mostly dark. A light had been left on in the kitchen, which made him hopeful.

He hurried to the back door and knocked. He waited impatiently, but Tegan didn't answer. He knocked again, shifting on the balls of his feet and turning his back to the cold wind. Maybe he was wrong after all.

When he still received no response, he tried the doorknob. Just in case. It turned easily and he felt a twinge of guilt as he stepped inside.

"Tegan?" he called out.

Where the devil was she? Leaving the lights on and the doors unlocked. Damn foolish thing to do. There was no telling who could just walk in.

"Teg—"

He stopped short as he stepped into the living room and saw her asleep on the couch. A quilt was pulled loosely around her shoulders and her hair fanned out on the pillows like a flow of molten gold. Her hand was curled under her cheek, her face soft and pale in the firelight.

Hoping he didn't frighten her too badly, he tiptoed over to the couch and put a gentle hand on her shoulder. "Tegan? Wake up."

She came awake with a gasp. "Steve!"

That was all she could manage as she sat up and threw off the quilt. Her sleep-fuddled brain didn't seem to want to kick into gear.

"Tegan, are you okay?"

"Fine. I just lay down for a nap."

"Would some coffee help you wake up?"

She started to say yes, then she remembered something she'd read about caffeine not being good for a developing fetus. "Um, no, thanks. I think I'll get a ginger ale out of the fridge."

"You stay put," he said, reinforcing the order by pushing her back down onto the couch as she tried to rise. "I'll get it for you."

As she finally cleared her head, her thoughts of him and her self-revelation rolled over her in a wave. Once again things were happening too fast. It served to remind her that she needed to steel herself against him. The mere sight of him had sent her pulse racing. She must not, could not, reveal any of the things she'd just been contemplating before her nap.

Accepting the cold can he offered upon his return, Tegan stared at Steve as he retreated across the room. Hiking his boot on the hearth, he leaned an elbow on the mantel and watched her back.

It seemed as if he were waiting for her to say something. Paradoxically, the longer he stared, the angrier she became. How dare he just come back and walk into the house as if he hadn't been gone for almost a month!

It was absurd, after the hours of self-examination and emotional upheaval she'd experienced to arrive at a modicum of peace, that one sight of him made it all for nothing. All her decisions, her well-thought-out motives...one look at his gorgeous face, his incredible body, and poof! Gone.

"What are you doing here?"

"Is it just me, or is there a distinct feeling of déjà vu here?"

Nothing would have made her admit he was right. "I don't think that's an answer to my question."

She could see him thinking, as if weighing his response.

"All right, try this one. I'm back. To stay. This is my ranch, this is my house. But I'm willing to share it with you."

"You can't stay here!"

"Why not?"

"Because... because... just because, that's why."

"Did you have a restraining order placed against me?"

She huffed. "You know I didn't do that. I didn't think I'd see your...your...no-good, low-down face again."

He smiled.

It infuriated her.

"No order, huh? Then you can't make me leave."

"I'll call the sheriff."

"Go ahead."

She reached for the phone and stopped in a disgusted huff when the receiver unit wasn't there. Where had she left the darn thing now? She glared at him and dared him to laugh.

She could see him struggling not to smile as he said, "Remember, I have a legitimate claim to this property that hasn't been decided by a court of law. What if the deputy is one of my friends, or a friend of my grandad's? What if they make *you* leave?"

Blast the man! Those were a lot of what-if's, but the bets were definitely hedged in his favor around here.

She gripped the edge of the cushion. "This really isn't fair, Steve." Her nails pressed so hard she threatened the fabric.

"You're right, it isn't."

Her shoulders dropped in resignation. "Steve, why are you here? Truthfully."

He moved across the room and gently pried her hand off the cushion to clasp it between his warm palms as he sat down beside her. "I have done nothing but think about you since the day I left. I couldn't get any work done, I couldn't play, I couldn't do anything because I couldn't get my mind off you."

She was glad she wasn't the only one who'd been off-balance this whole time. She arched an eyebrow at him but didn't respond.

"I want to start over, Tegan. Our lives were thrown together in a very bizarre way, but I think we might have a chance at something special between us. All I know is, I have to give it a try."

Her hand felt as though it were on fire, but the rest of her was trembling. It took everything she had to break the contact and move away. There was so much he didn't know. And she wasn't ready to tell him.

"Don't you think a little too much has happened for us to try the friendship bit?"

"I'm willing to start with friendship."

"Steve, that's not what I meant, and you know it."

He held up his hands. "I'm sorry. I didn't mean to be flip. The answer is, yes, I think a lot has happened between us in a very short time, but no, I don't think it's too much for us to get to know each other.''

''Couldn't you have simply called and asked me for a date?''

''Would you have gone?''

She looked at the floor.

''I guess that answers my question, doesn't it?'' Steve teased. ''Besides, don't you think the drive is a little long for the dating ritual?''

''Well, maybe, but you really shouldn't have just shown up on my doorstep like this.'' She put her hands on her hips. ''And how long were you planning on staying, anyway?''

''As long as it takes.''

''But what about the Navy? I know you get a lot of leave, but—''

''I resigned my commission.''

She gasped. ''Steve! What will you do? I mean, if this doesn't... if... I mean...''

''I have plenty of options, Tegan. I have a friend in the FBI who's been after me for years to join, although I've got to make that decision very quickly. I'm almost too old, if you can believe that. Or I could open a hardware store like my grandfather. Or I could give flying lessons—''

''How? I thought you were grounded.''

''I can't fly fighter jets but that doesn't mean I'm no longer a pilot.''

Tegan arched her eyebrows. ''Oh. I don't know why I got the impression they'd taken your license.''

''It's closer to being restricted—like when you have to wear glasses and they put that on your license. You still get to drive, but you have limitations.''

Her smile was wry. ''Thanks, Steve, but I think I could've figured it out.''

He blushed. She found that endearing.

''Sorry. I guess sometimes I feel like I have to convince people I'm still a good pilot.''

Tegan dimpled. ''Aviator.''

His returning grin was delighted. "Roger that."

She almost laughed out loud when Steve ran his fingers through his hair. At the same time, a strange feeling knotted in her stomach. She'd had no idea how much she missed watching him do that.

A silence fell between them and Tegan began to fidget. When she realized it, she became angry again. Anger and confusion seemed to be her two most prominent feelings where Steve was concerned, and then she added tired.

With great effort, she tried to regain some of her sense of humor. "Yet again, you and I have not stayed on task. We were talking about why you're here."

"And I thought I answered you."

"I feel more like you issued an edict. I don't recall any negotiation taking place."

"What is there to negotiate?"

His expression was much too innocent. Tegan wasn't going to fall for it. "Such as, maybe I'd like to try your plan and maybe I wouldn't, but you don't have the right to barge in here and stay." She gave him a hard look. "Lawsuit or no lawsuit."

Steve stood and paced, raising his hand to tap his finger on his lip. "It seems to me the art of successful negotiation is to take the one or two most important issues and resolve them. Agreed?"

Tegan bobbed her head in a slow nod. She had the distinct feeling she'd just lost ground somewhere.

"Then I submit that we look at issue number one, which is whether or not we should get to know each other better. Number two, we shall decide whether or not I stay here in the house, and after that, we won't sweat the small stuff."

"You think the lawsuit is the small stuff?"

"In the grand scheme of things, yes."

She shook her head despairingly.

"So—" He moved to her side and leaned his hands on the arm of the couch.

She had to arch her neck to look up at him but found, surprisingly, that she didn't mind at all. In fact, she thought she could look at him for hours and not get tired.

"Back to issue number one. I argue that our first encounters were less than auspicious." His voice dropped to a deeper level. "Well, not all of them. . . ."

She blushed, knowing he was thinking of the same thing she was, and that he'd fully intended to remind her.

"Tegan, our relationship deserves a chance to grow. I hope you feel the same way."

Hesitantly she agreed.

"Okay, then, that takes care of the biggest question. Now, number two was whether or not I'd stay here. I argue that if I stayed in town, valuable time and resources would be lost. Let us also consider that Ghost Dancer needs a place to stay, and I wouldn't even think of letting him visit with his new friend unless I took responsibility for his care. Are we in agreement so far?"

Tegan fought a smile as she sat back on the couch and crossed her arms over her chest. Inwardly she was already hoisting the white flag, but she couldn't wait to hear what he had to say next.

Twelve

Steve all but snapped imaginary suspenders and rocked on the balls of his feet as he said, "My last, and possibly most eloquent argument, is that the roads outside have a quarter inch of ice on them." Turning to face her squarely, he managed the most hangdog expression Tegan had ever seen. "You wouldn't send me out into that, would you?"

"Sorry, buster, the weather excuse was used up the first time. You've got a four-wheel-drive vehicle. You could make it to town if you wanted."

"That's just it," he smiled, a quirk of his mouth filled with humor and just a touch of wickedness, "I don't."

Tegan knew, beyond a shadow of a doubt, that it was utter folly to put herself in his proximity again. In light of her self-revelation, she wondered how she thought she could manage to keep her heart immune to Steve's charm. Just seeing him grin sent shivers up her spine. When his smiles faded and he got that whiskey-dark look in his eyes, she almost shuddered as her body remembered his every touch.

She still didn't understand why he was doing this. She didn't believe Steve had a devious bone in his body, so despite Enrique's impolite accusation, she refused to believe Steve was trying to romance the place out from under her.

So just what did he want? Could she believe that he truly wanted to get to know her? And if so, to what end? The lawsuit still hung over them like a dark cloud. Add to that the baby Steve didn't even know about yet. What purpose could this arrangement serve?

Then, somehow, a small voice cut through the cacophony in her mind. Couldn't she just take it slow and find out? Did she have to analyze everything to death? Couldn't she just "be" for a while? Be still. Be curious. Be accepting. Just for once?

"All right, Steve."

"All right?"

"You can stay." He started to bend toward her—for a hug, for a kiss, she wasn't sure. She put a hand out to hold him at bay. "But if you misbehave, that's it. Got it? Out on your heels."

He placed his hand over his heart. "On my honor, I swear I won't do one single thing you don't want me to."

Tegan decided to let that variation on a simple oath pass.

Steve told her to wait there while he retrieved the rest of his things and stabled Ghost Dancer. Still lethargic, she didn't argue yet another autocratic order from him. In fact, she didn't even challenge him as he came back in and added another log to the fire.

More proof that she was still flustered.

He moved to the opposite end of the couch and sat, turning sideways to rest his arm along the back. His fingers just reached her, and he toyed with a length of her hair.

Try as she might, she couldn't pull away from his touch or his gaze. The quiet stillness stretched between them.

"I really missed you, you know," he said softly.

She knew he wanted her to echo the sentiment, but enough caution resurged within her to make her hesitate.

Nothing substantial had changed. She was still deathly afraid of losing control of her life, her destiny. Those fears could not be dismissed with a few soft words, no matter how much those whispers drew at her soul.

She reminded herself that she had every right to be wary of him. After all, he'd done it to her again—barged into her life and turned it upside down.

So how could she explain the wish, deep in her soul, that he would pull her into his arms and kiss her until she couldn't think anymore, until she had no room for doubt, until her questions and fears melted under the heat of his desire?

Her disappointment was sharp when he dropped the strands of her hair he'd been running through his fingers. She'd seen him shifting his position, trying discreetly to get comfortable, so she knew he was as affected as she was.

"Steve, I—"

The phone rang, making her jump. She made a face at Steve when he laughed at her as she reached again for the receiver that wasn't there. His grin broadened as she hit the speaker button with a disgusted sigh.

"Hey, Tegan."

Tegan glanced at Steve quickly. "Angelica, listen, I can't talk. Steve's here."

Angelica gasped. "He is? Have you told him about the baby?"

Tegan moaned. She couldn't believe what had just happened! "No, but you just did. You're on the speaker."

"Oh, no! Tegan, I'm so sorry."

"I've got to go. I'll call you later."

She sat frozen on the couch. Dear God, what was she going to do now? Her eyes followed him as Steve slowly got off the couch and resumed his earlier position by the fireplace. Her heart felt like it was beating a hundred miles an hour and she was only able to take shallow, panting breaths.

"Do you want to explain that call to me?" Steve asked, his face void of expression, his voice evenly moderated.

She was all too aware that he was not making a request.

"It seems pretty obvious to me," she said, a returning sense of defiance melting her frozen limbs. "I'm pregnant."

Slowly he raised his eyes to hers. "Then I can assume, since Angelica asked if you'd told me, that the baby is mine?"

"That's a safe assumption."

"I thought you told me you and your ex-husband tried for years to have a baby and that you couldn't."

Heaven knew that was the truth! Hadn't she asked God a thousand times, why now?

"I did tell you that. And I always thought it was my fault. My ex told me he'd gotten a girl pregnant when he was a teenager and the girl had lost the baby so since I knew he could get someone pregnant, it seemed a logical conclusion that I was infertile."

"But you were never tested."

"No. We kept thinking it would happen soon. Then our marriage got strained and we were having sex so infrequently it was little surprise that I didn't get pregnant. Then we separated, so there didn't seem to be any point."

She relaxed a little when he moved to the rocker by the fireplace and sat heavily. He pressed his hands against his face, rubbing at his temples as though fighting a headache.

In her heart of hearts she knew he would never hurt her, but he'd looked so threatening when he'd stood across the room from her, his face set as though etched in stone. Maybe he didn't realize how intimidating he was when drawn to full height, muscles taut, his expression cold.

When he looked up, she felt some of the tension leave her stomach. With just the slightest easing of the muscles in his face, his eyes no longer seemed to chill her.

"Tegan, I will do the right thing by you. We can get married as soon as possible."

"Oh, we can?" Tegan was incredulous. "And just what makes you think I want to marry you?"

"It is the right thing to do, Tegan. I will give you, and our child, my name."

"Well, I don't need your name. I don't need anything from you."

Steve's mouth tightened but she continued before he could say anything more. "I'm not one of your soldiers, Steve. You can't make me do anything. Certainly, you can't make me marry you. I don't need your outdated code of chivalry."

"There's nothing outmoded about being responsible, Tegan. It may be out of fashion in today's society, but it's not wrong."

"It would be wrong for us to commit to a relationship solely on the basis of a pregnancy. It would be no favor to the child. What if we ended up hating each other and made each other miserable?"

"And what if we ended up loving each other to distraction? There's no way to know unless we try. Tegan, we could make it work."

She doubted he could know that that was exactly the wrong thing to say to her. "I will never—understand this—never force myself into a relationship based on duty."

"Good relationships have been started on less."

Tegan forced a laugh. "You've got to be kidding! We've only been in each other's presence less than a week's worth of days and all we do is argue. Isn't that a pretty good indication that we're not exactly a dream match?"

"I don't think we have enough information to form a conclusion about what kind of relationship we could have. The circumstances that brought us together are unusual, I admit—"

"Unusual is a nice way of putting it!"

Steve dropped his head into his hands again and Tegan kept her tongue.

She was taken off guard when he jerked his head out of his hands and pinned her with a glance.

"How long have you known?"

She swallowed. She hadn't expected that question. "Just under two weeks."

"When were you going to tell me?"

Her chin came up as her tone became deliberately more defiant. "I'm not sure that I ever was. I hadn't made that decision yet."

"What were you going to do? Get rid of it?"

"This is the nineties. That was one of my options."

She watched him snap that rigid control back into place, and she felt her pulse speed up again.

She looked away and back again. "It may be crazy, considering the circumstances, but I want my baby."

She almost smiled when she watched him rise from the chair and pace away from her, execute a perfect 180-degree turn and set his feet apart at parade rest. She had the absurd urge to salute him.

But there was absolutely nothing funny about the look in his eyes. It was a look that told her he would brook no dissimulation from her.

"I don't agree that trying to work things out between us is futile."

"I guess we'll just have to agree to disagree."

That hard look came back into his eyes.

"Maybe, but you need to understand this—I won't let you keep my child from me. You have no right to do that."

"Don't talk to me about rights, Steve Williams! I have a right to run my life the way I want to. I have a right to my own best destiny. I have a right to be happy and live without some overbearing, pompous jerk telling me what to do with everything from my home to my body!"

"Pompous? You think I'm pompous?"

"At the very least, yes."

"You don't know squat about me, Tegan. If you did, you'd know that what I am right now is scared." He frowned at her obvious disbelief. "Yes, scared. Out-of-my-wits frightened that you would take this baby, and my child would grow up without a father. Incomplete."

Just like I did. He didn't say the words but they hung like smoke in the air between them.

"I—I didn't think about that."

"You didn't think about what single parenthood would entail?" His voice betrayed his incredulence.

"Of course I did. I just thought that I could be a good enough mother to make up for it."

"I've known lots of single parents in my time in the military. Both moms and dads. And yes, they do try twice as hard, and they do damn good jobs raising their kids, but I don't know of a kid out there who doesn't want two parents."

"What about kids with abusive homes?"

"We're not going to debate the relative miseries of our society right now, Tegan. Of course there are kids out there much better off being with just one parent, but that doesn't mean in their dreams and prayers they don't ask for a good mom or dad to replace the defective one."

"All right, all right. I concede the point. Every child deserves to know both parents."

She doubted he knew how bleak his look turned. It made her heart ache when he whispered, "I'd have given anything to know even one."

The old Steve returned instantly, as though aware of his break of form. His shoulders straightened back and his voice turned hard again. "I'll be damned if a child of mine will grow up without me."

"I said all right, didn't I?" Her fingers clutched at the back of the cushions. "Now that you know, I'd never deny you visitation."

Something flashed in his eyes. It made her shiver.

"As you so aptly pointed out, this is the nineties. What if I get custody and *you* get the visitation?"

Her heart stopped in her chest. Her blood turned to ice in her veins. Her lungs ached as though pressed in a vise and her stomach knotted. She wrapped her arms over her abdomen in an instinctive reaction.

"You wouldn't," she whispered, horrified.

Steve rubbed his eyes wearily. It wasn't until he looked at her that she could breathe again.

"Tegan, I'm sorry. I should never have said that. That was cruel and I ask your forgiveness."

She couldn't respond. She darn sure couldn't say that it was all right. It wasn't. Nothing she'd ever experienced came close to that moment of paralyzing fear of even contemplating the loss of her child. Her agonizing loneliness after the divorce, the fear of losing the ranch—they were pale imitations of that gut-wrenching sensation. And she prayed she never felt it again as long as she lived.

Steve seemed unaware of her turmoil when he continued. She hoped so. To know he could affect her so profoundly would give him even more power over her than he already knew he had. She couldn't risk that.

"While I don't believe that being female automatically qualifies women as the better parent, no, I wouldn't do that to you. I hate the thought of mere visitation, but I will be an integral part of my child's life." He looked as though he was trying valiantly to smile. "I don't know how, but I know you'll be a great mom."

Taking her first full breath in what seemed like hours, Tegan managed an acknowledging nod. "Thank you."

A long, tense silence filled the room. Neither one of them could think of what else to say in the moment. Finally, Steve moved toward the stairs and his duffel bag lying at the bottom.

"I'm going to go unpack."

"Fine. I'll start some supper, if you're hungry."

"That would be great. Thanks."

Steve climbed the stairs slowly, his head reeling with everything that had just transpired.

A baby! Jeez, how could it be. One time! The one and only time he had ever made love to a woman without protection and she gets pregnant.

A long time ago he had vowed that he would never bring a child into this world. He made that decision based on his childhood and the fact that he had a risky job that would have kept him away from a family for months on end. Yes, he'd grown up loved and cared for, but a part of him would never get over that feeling of abandonment, of knowing his parents didn't want him. Since he never intended to be anything but a pilot and career Navy man, he'd decided that the white picket fence, the dog, and the kid thing would never be his. That was a trade-off he'd been willing to make and he'd insured that it had never happened.

Throwing his bag into the room, Steve bounced backward onto the bed and stacked his hands under his head. He stared at the ceiling with unseeing eyes.

A baby!

If that wasn't a twist he hadn't been expecting, he didn't know what one was.

So, all things considered, did this change how he felt about her? Two hours ago he'd been in love with her, remember?

He had to swallow hard around the lump in his throat to answer honestly: he wasn't sure. Until this moment he hadn't considered that somewhere in the back of his mind he had taken comfort in the knowledge the Tegan couldn't have children. He hadn't put it into thought, but he realized part of his attraction to Tegan was that very fact. He didn't want to have to face parenthood, especially his deep-seated fears about his ability to be a father, so he'd chosen a woman who, he thought, would never force him to make that decision.

It had been so much easier when he'd thought the matter was out of his hands.

The truth was, it *was* out of his hands now. He was going to be a father whether he liked it or not.

But he did like it. He was scared, yes, but some deep part of him was jumping for joy now that the initial shock had worn off.

A baby!

Could he do it? Could he be a father? Better still, could he be a dad? Did he have it in him?

Steve bounded out of bed and hurried downstairs. It soothed his ego to tell himself that he wasn't running from his thoughts but instead was being polite to Tegan. He shouldn't keep her waiting any longer.

He stopped inside the kitchen doorway, once more taken aback by her beauty. He thought he could stand there and drink in the sight of her until time stood still.

She was standing at the stove, wearing a frilly apron incongruous with her work shirt and jeans, stirring something in a pot. The scene was so homey, so domestic, for a moment that old fear assailed him again, reminding him that this was what he had always known could never be his.

And, in truth, it still might not be. He had no guarantee that things would work out for the best between Tegan and him. The force of his wishing wouldn't necessarily make things come true.

It hurt too badly to even contemplate leaving her, leaving here. Where would he go? What would he do? For the first time, the uncertainty of his own future nearly knocked him over.

He must have made some noise, for Tegan glanced over her shoulder at him.

"Ready? I'm afraid it's not very elegant, but it's hearty."

"Smells great."

"It's just homemade vegetable soup and grilled sandwiches. I hope you don't mind."

"Of course not. You aren't obligated to feed me, Tegan."

She paused as she set the plate of sandwiches on the table. "I know that. But to be honest, cooking keeps my hands busy so that I don't go crazy."

That he could understand.

They ate in strained silence. Unable to stand it any longer, he reached across the table and touched the back of her hand. "Tegan, I have to say again how sorry I am for what I said. I didn't mean to frighten you."

Tegan clasped his hand for a quick second before disengaging the contact. "I accept your apology, Steve. This situation is just as disconcerting to me as it is to you."

She toyed with her soup. He sensed she wanted to say something more so he stayed quiet.

"Steve . . ." She swallowed as though it was difficult. "I didn't mean to hurt you, either. I was going to tell you about the baby. I just wasn't ready yet."

He nodded slowly. "I'm trying to understand, trying to put myself in your shoes. I guess if you'll do the same, we'll get past the hurt."

The rest of the meal felt lighter, but nothing could have surprised him more than when Tegan dropped her spoon and burst out laughing.

She giggled until tears began to stream down her face. Steve started to worry that she'd gone a little crazy when she held up a hand and shook her head, finally getting herself under control.

"I'm sorry, Steve," she gasped, catching her breath. "It's just, all of a sudden, it hit me that every moment you and I have been together has been a monumentally emotional event. Then I remembered that I left the city for peace and quiet, and the absurdity of everything that's happened just kind of bowled me over."

Steve felt his own lips twitch and before he knew it, he was laughing right along with her.

It felt so good that the tension seemed to dissipate like clouds against a strong wind. And suddenly, where he'd been forcing himself to eat out of politeness before, his appetite returned and he dug into his meal with a gusto.

It was much later, when they were back in the living room with a cheery fire blazing in the fireplace, that the serious tone returned to their conversation.

"Steve?"

"Hmm?" he answered, not taking his eyes off the flames.

"Can I ask you something?"

"That's a silly question, under the circumstances."

"Humor me," she said dryly.

"Yes, you can ask me a question," he responded dutifully.

"I've been thinking and I got a little confused. Weren't the Williamses your mother's parents?"

"Yes."

"But your name is Williams. You didn't take your dad's name?"

"My birth certificate says 'father unknown.'"

"Oh." She paused. "I'm sorry. I didn't mean to bring up unpleasant memories."

"It's all right. You have a right to know about our child's heritage."

Steve kept his gaze focused on the fire for a long, long time. For all his avowals of intending to be an active father, for all that he was deadly earnest, there was a place in the back of his mind that mocked him, asking him how he could be capable of loving a child when his own father hadn't loved him.

"My mother," he began dispassionately, "was always something of a wild child. My grandfather never talked about her, but my grandmother told me some details as I was growing up. She never understood what she did wrong, and nothing could convince Gran that my mother's rebellion wasn't her fault."

Stretching his legs out and leaning back, Steve locked his fingers together over his stomach.

"I know my grandparents weren't perfect, and I guess if anything, they were guilty of being too loving. Gran admitted they spoiled my mother rotten. She left home to see the world, and never came back. Except to dump me on the doorstep."

Tegan let the silence linger for a long time.

"If you're anything like me," she began hesitantly, "you're wondering if we'll do any better a job than our folks did. I'm worried I'll be just like my mother."

Rolling his head on the cushion to look at her, he held her eyes for a long time. "That's very perceptive of you. I was just considering whether I'll be able to be any better a parent than mine were."

She sighed. "I try to remember that my folks did the best they could and in the end, I am not my mother. I'm sure I'll make mistakes, but things will be different."

Steve nodded. "And I reminded myself that my grandfather, for all his faults, was a great role model. If I take his example and build on it, I'll do fine."

Tegan smiled. "I'm really glad we kept talking. It would have been much easier to retreat to our rooms in stony silence."

"I'm glad we did, too. In fact, I'd guess we have a lot to talk about."

"It's amazing how much, yet how little we know about each other."

Steve reached over and stroked his fingers down the velvety softness of her cheek. "And I'd like to get to know you, Tegan. I want to know everything about you."

Slowly, so that she had all the time in the world to protest, he leaned down to kiss her. Just one, he promised himself. Just a sip of the sweet nectar that was her taste alone. Just one caress to prove to himself that there was hope, that a spark still remained between them that could be fanned to life again.

She sighed against his lips when they finally met. Her fingers reached up to rest in the curve of his neck, her thumb caressing his jaw. Her lips parted and he knew that jolting excitement when their tongues melded.

Soon, too soon. He wanted her. Now. But there was too much to risk, too much to lose by hurrying.

With every ounce of strength he possessed, he forced himself to press his lips to hers one last time and back away.

"We're doing it again." He couldn't keep the husky, passionate tone from his voice.

She smiled impishly. "Really? I thought we were just kissing."

He gave her a teasing, scolding look. "Stop that."

She knew she was the one who had set the boundaries, but for the first time in as long as she could remember, she was feeling playful. She tried to look contrite and failed. "Yes, sir."

"Tegan," he said, amused exasperation slipping in, "we've got to slow down!" He took her face in his hands and kissed her eyes, her nose, her cheeks, and finally her mouth. "I want you more than anything on this earth right now. But we both know we need to wait, to take that time we said we needed to get to know each other."

She leaned back, heaving a disappointed sigh. "I know. You're right." She rolled her head back toward him. "But I don't have to like it."

With a chuckle, Steve stood. "Neither do I. And on that note, I'm going to go to bed. If I don't, we'll both regret it."

The devilish smile was back. "Maybe not."

He bent over and placed a kiss on her forehead. "Good night, Tegan," he said firmly.

"'Night."

When he was safely upstairs, she added petulantly, "But I don't know how good it'll be."

Thirteen

Tegan brewed herself some decaf tea and sat down at the table, trying to wake up. She grimaced at her cup. What she really wanted was a giant mug of strong coffee and it was making her cranky.

For the past week, she and Steve had talked until all hours of the night. Yet no matter how late they stayed awake, Steve was always up and about early the next morning. When she heard him knocking around, she inevitably rolled over and pulled a pillow over her head until she couldn't take it anymore. Then she forced herself downstairs to sit at the table, half-comatose and trying to revive.

Last night had been worse than most. Unable to sleep, despite the ungodly hour she'd crawled into bed, she'd snuck back downstairs and built the fire up again. She'd worked for hours on her new creation, trying to tire herself out so she could sleep. But the more she'd thought about her quilt, the more she'd tried to picture Steve's grandmother. And the more she pictured what the woman might have been like, the more she'd thought of Steve. She imagined him as he might have been as a young boy, then a teenager, then a young man. At one point she'd gotten up, fixed herself some hot chocolate and returned to the couch.

And burst into tears.

She loved him. Irrationally, illogically, she loved him and couldn't pretend any longer that she didn't. She thought she had probably been infatuated with him from the first moment she'd seen his pictures, and then fallen head-over-heels the instant he'd burst through her door.

She didn't care that it didn't make sense, that people would say it was impossible to fall in love that fast. Or maybe they'd say she was manufacturing the feeling because of the baby.

The fact was undeniable.

And she didn't know what to do. This past week had been wonderful—talking, laughing, playing. Getting to know Steve on a deeper and deeper level. He still infuriated her when he got autocratic—like telling her she couldn't ride her horse until after the baby was born. Or not letting her handle the cat because of something he'd read somewhere about pregnant women avoiding cats. Or not letting her go outside when the sleet got bad because she might slip.

Yet some part of her would not let go that he wouldn't be so solicitous if it wasn't for the baby. Then the other part of her brain would remind her that he'd come back before he'd known about the baby. Around and around the argument would go in her mind, until she thought she would go crazy. She wanted Steve to fall in love with her, for who and what she was. She didn't want a commitment from him out of pity or duty.

And there was one thing she was absolutely sure of—Steve had an overabundant sense of duty.

Reaching for her cup, she took a sip and nearly cursed when she burned her tongue. Putting the steaming cup down, she took a bite of sweet roll instead. It didn't matter that they were the kind kept in the refrigerator in a can, then dropped onto cookie sheets to bake, the fact remained that Steve had made them and drizzled the icing generously over the ones he'd left for her.

He wasn't making it very easy to stay distant.

Tegan winced as the pounding started in the storeroom. In one of her bouts of mad cleaning, she had gotten it painted, but not put back together. Steve was now hammering enthusiastically as he remounted the shelves. He was so excited about helping around the house, she didn't have the heart to tell him to stop.

Good heavens, the man even went down the road to the mailbox every day and got the mail! Somehow, though, she knew Steve wasn't putting on an act. This was normal behavior for him.

She still wasn't sure what his strategy was, but if frustrating her was part of his plan, it was working perfectly. Every night, as they'd paused in the hall before going to their rooms, she had expected him to kiss her. But every night he stopped with her by her door, smiled sweetly, and either stroked her cheek with his thumb or squeezed her shoulder. And nothing more.

She knew this was the nineties. She knew she could be the aggressor, but she also knew that Steve was of the old guard—not only an officer and a gentleman, but a Southern gentleman. It was instinctive, but she was positive he wanted to make the first move.

At least, it was easier to tell herself that than to have to make a decision about being forward. Perhaps she was still too much of a Southern lady.

She snorted softly.

It had only been a week and she wasn't far from grabbing him the next time he walked by and ripping his clothes from his body. She kept a tenuous control on herself, though, but a little voice warned her that he'd better make a move soon.

Steve drove a nail into the stud and tossed the hammer to the floor. He was working up a sweat, but it was a good thing for him to keep busy. He could hear Tegan in the kitchen, and he forced himself to concentrate.

It had only been a week and he was pretty sure he was losing his mind. Every night they'd stayed up, talking about anything and everything imaginable. He'd told her about his childhood and about the Navy, and she'd told him about her childhood, about college, getting married, divorced, her career. He'd been fascinated.

And he'd been even more fascinated by the light as it played across her skin and became captured in her hair. By the smell of her skin—

He shook his head and pulled his thoughts back in line. What else had they talked about? Oh, yes—the holidays.

He'd been delighted to hear she'd planned to stay home this year. She'd said she didn't feel up to a visit to her parents' and she'd mentioned her friends Enrique and Angelica. He'd released a silent sigh when she'd gone on to say that the celebrations at the Esquivel household tended to be a little more than she cared for. So they'd decided to spend it together.

He had high hopes for Christmas.

Working steadily for another hour, he had most of the support boards up and ready for the shelves. He glanced at his watch, but it was too early to get the mail. Every day he checked the box, but the items hadn't come from his attorney.

He'd given in to a blinding passion with Tegan once, and while every moment spent alone with her was a temptation almost beyond endurance, he was determined to wait until he could be with her free of any shadows.

He wanted those papers. And soon.

Tegan wielded the scrub brush across the bathtub with a vengeance. Most of the second week had passed as pleasantly as the first, but it seemed as if all Steve and she had done for the past few days was snap at each other. Rather than bite his head off, she'd chosen to do housework, something she usually despised.

She'd glanced downstairs and seen that Steve was putting as much energy into buffing the hardwood floors as she was on the sinks and tub.

She knew it was shrewish, but she didn't think he had the right to be as mad as she was. After all, this was all his fault.

A breeze fluttered the curtain window and she sighed. The weather had been typical for this time of year, icy one minute, almost summery a few days later. Today was a summery one, the temperature about seventy, sunlight streaming down from the sky. Ghost Dancer and Dream Chaser seemed like the only ones appreciating it as they grazed contentedly in the pasture.

Tegan threw the brush into the tub. That was it. She'd had enough.

After washing her hands, she went into her bedroom and called Angelica to make plans for lunch. They set a time and place, and Tegan dressed.

Steve turned off the buffer when she walked by. "Going somewhere?"

"Not that it's any of your business, but I'm going into Austin for the afternoon."

His jaw tightened. "I didn't say it was my business, I was just trying to be polite."

Tegan didn't respond to the gibe. "I'll be back around seven or so."

Steve merely nodded and returned to his task. When she was gone, he shut the machine off with a swift kick to the power button.

He and Tegan had done nothing but snap at each other for days. The weather had changed to beautiful at the first of the week, so he couldn't blame the short tempers on cabin fever.

He could blame frustration, though.

Deciding Tegan's idea of getting out was a good one, he grabbed a couple of apples and headed toward the pasture.

After offering a consolation apple to Dream Chaser for being left behind, it only took him a few minutes to get Ghost Dancer saddled.

Taking his time, Steve rode around, letting Ghost Dancer run here, walk there. It helped clear his head. When he was ready, he stopped by the mailbox, ready to be disappointed again.

He wasn't.

There, in a large brown envelope, were the documents from his attorney. He looked down at the order and had the oddest mixture of feelings. He knew he'd done the right thing, what he'd wanted to do, but seeing the judge's signature made his stomach tighten for a moment. No matter what happened between Tegan and himself, the ranch was hers.

Yet, seeing the order also gave him a new sense of freedom. He'd restrained himself for two weeks now, not touching her, not kissing her, not pressuring her in any way. Now he could give her the papers and he could let her know how she affected him without feeling like he was manipulating her.

His pulse jumped at the very thought. Finally, he could take her into his arms with no guilt, for she wouldn't be able to doubt his intentions.

But it also meant she would have no reservations about turning him down, either, if she was so inclined. That was the very reason he had waited to pursue her romantically until he had the order. Otherwise, no matter what he said, there would always be doubt in her mind that he had ulterior motives. Now she would know he did not, and she had all the power.

He had hoped that these two weeks would show her that they had something special together, that they were compatible. These past few days had made him wonder, though. His mind went back and forth, convincing himself one minute that all couples had times of high tension—he'd just never stayed around long enough to experience them in the past. The next minute he'd tell himself it was stupid to put himself through this. He should just cut and run.

And oddly enough, he was sure that he wasn't sticking around for the baby's sake. Yes, he wanted to be a father to that child, but he wanted to stay because he loved Tegan.

For the first time, though, as he held the papers in his hands, he was glad he'd see it through. Whatever the outcome, he was going to give this his best shot. He loved her, and now he could make love with her without any clouds hanging over them.

His spirit revived as he headed back to the house. She said she'd be back around seven. That would give him plenty of time to put his plan into action.

Tegan headed west into the fading sunset. She had thought spending time with Angelica would make her feel better.

It hadn't. Angelica hadn't shut up about Steve, about how exciting this was, had he kissed her yet, had they made love again, what had he said about the baby... until Tegan had nearly screamed.

Angelica had not agreed with Tegan's argument as to why she couldn't let Steve know she loved him. Angelica had been adamant that hiding her feelings was wrong, regardless of what happened about the ranch, or the baby.

Tegan pulled into the yard and looked at the house. It seemed so cheery and welcoming. As she looked around, she knew a comforting peace. Yet she knew that her security no longer lay in this piece of property. It was important to her, yes, and would always hold a special place in her heart, but the idea that she could move on had become a solid conviction.

She was sure her soul could survive losing the ranch. Whether she'd ever get over Steve was another question entirely.

Shaking away her maudlin turn of thoughts, Tegan gathered her packages and headed into the house. The sight that greeted her made her stop in her tracks.

Steve was standing with his hands resting on the top of a chair at the opposite end of the table. Linen, china and crystal had been set, and a huge bouquet of yellow roses sat off center. Two yellow candles rose from silver holders, their wicks freshly lit. Soft music played on the stereo.

Steve spread his hands as he moved toward her. "I had to do it. The quintessential romantic dinner."

Tegan relinquished her packages to him as she took off her coat. She stared at him for what felt like forever. Something was different. It was in his face. A lightness, a certainty, a decision of some kind. . . .

She finally found her voice. "What's the occasion, Steve?"

"Not yet. No rushing. Why don't you sit down and I'll get you something to drink." A wary look came into his eyes. "You didn't eat in town, did you?"

Shaking her head, she reassured him, "Not since lunch."

"Good."

She sat as instructed, fingering the cool blossoms of the roses. He must have paid a fortune for the two dozen or so out-of-season blooms gracing the table. Most were just opening, but one or two buds were still tightly layered closed. With her eyes shut, she breathed in the heady perfume.

As she sipped the fruit drink Steve had brought her, she felt herself relaxing. She watched him move around the kitchen and knew the warmth spreading through her wasn't from the heater. Every time she looked at him she experienced the same sensation.

Warned once, she wasn't about to ask again, but she wanted him to hurry. When he dimmed the lights and made the setting doubly romantic, she couldn't enjoy it completely. She even found herself rushing through the delicious chicken Alfredo he'd placed in front of her.

Steve remained infuriatingly polite and calm. He asked her about her day, chatted about his, and, in general, was a charming dinner companion.

She started to fidget. She didn't say anything, but was grateful when he had pity on her, took her hand, and led her to the living room. Waiting expectantly, she clasped her hands in front of her as she moved to the couch.

"Tegan, I won't draw this out any longer. I just wanted to have the perfect setting to give you this."

He reached over and handed her some folded papers she hadn't noticed lying on the coffee table. With trembling fingers, she opened them. She sat there, stunned, as she read the order.

She finally reached the bottom and looked at the date.

"You didn't tell me. All this time and you didn't tell me."

"I meant what I said when I got here, Tegan. I wanted to spend time with you and I didn't want you letting me stay out of some kind of misguided gratitude. Or even for the baby's sake."

She turned the corners of her mouth up wryly. "Or maybe you thought I wouldn't believe you?"

He shrugged one shoulder. "And maybe that, too."

"Of all the things I thought about during dinner, I could never have imagined this."

Steve stroked his fingertips over her brow. "I'd love to hear what you did imagine."

She blushed, hating the heat she could feel rising from her neck. Toying with the edges of the paper, she avoided his question and finally glanced up.

"I don't know what to say about this. I'm stunned."

"I don't need you to say anything. It might take a while to sink in."

Her capacity for honesty surfaced once again. "I have to tell you that I was walking around rather proud of myself because I had decided to take your offer and let you have the ranch back."

Steve stared at her. "Really? Why?"

Her capacity did not include admitting she loved him yet. "Because this is your birthright. You have more than twenty years of memories here. I have less than one."

"That doesn't make your memories any less valid."

"No, but I came to realize that it isn't the memories that are important to me. It's the growth I've achieved. I can grow anywhere. It's not tied to this piece of land."

She looked at him and suddenly chuckled. "So what do we do now? I've cut off my hair, and you've sold your watch."

"Pardon?" Then his expression cleared. "Oh, I remember that story," he said, and joined her in the laughter.

Their voices quieted, and he moved closer to frame her face with his hands. "I won't speak for you, but my gift is from my heart."

Her eyelids fluttered shut. "Oh, Steve, just kiss me."

His mouth moved over hers reverently. She sighed against his lips. It had been so long, but now it seemed worth the agony of waiting.

She leaned into him, needing to feel his arms around her. The kiss changed, becoming hungry. Tangling her fingers in his hair, she pulled him closer.

She didn't think she could ever get enough of this. His tongue battled with hers, his fingers stroked her face and neck. Time went on and on as they reacquainted themselves with the taste and touch of each other.

When the frenzied kisses finally slowed, it took her a moment to realize that Steve was gently disentangling her arms from around him and moving back.

She was shocked, dismayed, disappointed. Embarrassed. Her face heated as she thought of how abandoned her behavior had been.

"Steve?"

"Don't misunderstand," he whispered, his voice deep and husky with desire as his thumb traced her kiss-swollen lips. "I want you so badly I ache. But you're reeling right now from everything that's happened, and I will not take advantage of you."

It finally sank in. He wasn't going to make love with her! How noble. How gentlemanly. How frustrating!

Tegan hated to admit that, in part, he was right. She was a little dazed. She had wanted to be the generous one, the gift-giver. And he'd beaten her to it.

He had thought she wouldn't believe his lovemaking was honest because the property issue wasn't settled. Now he wouldn't believe she wanted to make love with him because the property issue *was* settled.

What a perfectly lovely catch-22.

But how long could she wait to know him again?

Tentatively, another blush heating her face, she snuggled her cheek into his hand. "How can I convince you that I want you?"

"I believe you, but I don't want there to be regrets between us again. It would be a mistake to move too fast now. We've waited this long, let's give ourselves time to settle in."

"That sounds so logical. So agonizingly, frustratingly logical."

He chuckled softly. "I'm beginning to wonder who said it, because I'm about to go crazy wanting to touch you."

"How long are you going to torture us?"

"Christmas is just over two weeks away...." he said tentatively.

She could make it to Christmas, couldn't she? It seemed so important to him.

"Okay, Christmas it is."

Steve had never imagined two weeks dragging by so slowly, nor flying by so swiftly. Yet once they'd made their pact, a new dimension had been added to their relationship.

When Tegan would walk by, he could grab her now and pull her down for a kiss, or swat her bottom, or take her hand. She would laugh and move into his arms for a hug, or return a kiss, or pinch his behind.

They'd gotten a tree and decorated it from top to bottom. Amazingly, without the other ever seeing, presents began to pile up on the tree skirt. It had become a game to see who could come up with the most bizarre reasons for needing to go into town, and how they could sneak their packages in without the other the wiser.

He had never had so much fun in his life.

Every shop he went by had something he couldn't resist. He'd bought everything from a crystal hummingbird that attached to the window by a suction cup to a beaded sweater he couldn't wait to see on her gorgeous body. His final gift had been picked up this morning and was waiting in the barn.

Evenings were heavenly torture. They sat on the couch and cuddled and necked like teenagers. Sometimes they just sat in silence with her head on his chest as he played with her hair.

It was a wonderful time of discovery. Tegan said again and again how special she felt, how appreciated. He'd echoed the words, for he felt the same. It was something he had never experienced before.

The only niggling worry he had left was that when the time came and he spoke of his love, that she wouldn't, or couldn't, say the words back to him. He knew his fear was irrational—he could see her responses to him in her eyes. But he still wouldn't be sure until he heard the words from her own perfect lips.

He thought of his gift and could hardly wait for tomorrow morning. He'd spent a lot of time in the barn today, and he hoped she didn't suspect.

Christmas morning came and Steve jumped out of bed like an excited child. His only concession to the cold and to modesty was to tug on a pair of new, satin pajama pants. He threw the matching robe over his shoulders as he bounded down the hall to knock on her door. He didn't wait for an answer and went in to sit beside her, bouncing on the bed.

"Stop it," came Tegan's muffled command from under her pillow. She was lying on her stomach with her face buried in the bed.

"Wake up, sleepyhead. It's Christmas!"

"Let it be Christmas later."

Steve slapped her beautiful derriere.

"Ouch!"

"Get up."

"Don't want to."

"Then it's war." He tickled her unmercifully until she squealed with indignant laughter.

"Okay, okay! I give!" She tried for a grouchy expression. "How could I go back to sleep now anyway?"

"Let's go downstairs and see what Santa brought."

Despite her earlier lethargy, Tegan now could hardly contain her excitement as she rushed through her morning routine. After brushing her teeth, she pulled her hair back and braided it quickly out of her way. Then she pulled on her robe and started carrying the boxes downstairs while Steve was outside.

He said he had to run to the barn, so she waited on the couch. She looked up expectantly when he returned, but was surprised that he was empty-handed. Shrugging her confusion away, she carefully nudged the bottom box into its place.

Everything was perfect. Spiced cider was heating in the Crock-Pot, the fire Steve had built before he'd gone outside crackled, Bing Crosby was singing "White Christmas," and they were ready to begin.

"Tegan—"

"Steve," she interrupted, despite his obvious eagerness, "I want to go first."

Reluctantly he nodded.

She took a deep breath. "These aren't really presents from me, since they have always been yours, but I wanted to wait until today to give them to you. I hope you don't mind."

Steve accepted the large box she handed him, but it wasn't until he looked at the other eight stacked at her feet that he made the connection.

"Gran's quilts!"

He opened the top as he spoke, his voice fading as he slowly unfolded the special acid-free paper that surrounded the quilt. The expression on his face softened even more as he ran his hand over the creation. Tegan would have sworn she saw a tear in his eye.

"I never thought I'd see this again," he whispered.

Tegan glanced at the box and sat down beside him. "You know, when I found these in the trunk in the attic, I pulled them out and ached because I knew there were precious stories behind them that I knew I would never hear."

Steve smiled. "This is my chicken pox quilt."

Tegan kicked off her house slippers and pulled her feet onto the couch, wrapping her arms around her legs as she prepared to listen to his memories. She didn't know who was more excited, Steve or her, when he spread the quilt over his lap and most of the couch. He smoothed the fabric under his palm.

"When I was nine," Steve continued, "I got a bad case of the chicken pox. I was miserable. There wasn't much that could keep a nine-year-old occupied, and there's only so much television a kid can watch, so Gran decided to enlist my help before I drove us both crazy."

"Ah! That explains it."

Steve cocked his head at her. "Explains what?"

She hesitated. "I could tell that this quilt had not been done entirely by your grandmother. The color placement and skill in the blocks aren't up to her usual standards."

"Hey! I thought I did pretty good on this thing."

"Actually, you did. But you didn't have your grandmother's talent with a needle, or her eye for color. It is just so endearing to know that she let you do what you wanted, not making you conform to anyone's scheme but your own, and then she took as much care in the quilting as on any of her other works.''

Steve chuckled. "Yeah, I was well before it was time to complete it, but Gran didn't put it away." He traced around a triangle with his fingertip. "Do you know that I slept with this for years?"

Tegan nodded. "I didn't know what bed this was put on, of course, but you can tell that it has been used. Lovingly used, but this is no touch-me-not quilt." She put her hand on his arm. "Do you know what this pattern is called?"

His forehead furrowed as he tried to remember. "It had something to do with flying, I know that." He grinned. "I guess I was destined for the sky from the beginning."

"It's called Flying Geese. I wasn't surprised when I read the inscription block on the back that she'd done it for you." She flipped the end of the quilt over and showed him the hand-embroidered block that said To My Stevie. With Love, Gran. "Steve, you are so lucky."

He looked at her, not the quilt, when he said, "Yes, I know."

She dropped her eyes, suddenly flustered. She handed him the next box, and Tegan listened, fascinated, as the stories unfolded.

Soon they were opening each other's presents. Tegan couldn't remember ever being more delighted with Christmas. Steve seemed to be having more fun watching her than opening his own gifts, and she basked in his affection.

It wasn't until he made her promise not to peek and left the room that the tiniest uncertainty crept into her heart.

Why couldn't she get rid of these last doubts? He'd said he loved her with his eyes a hundred times already. What more did she need? She wished she could just let go and say the words aloud.

"Ready?" Steve called from the doorway.

"Yep."

"Are your eyes closed?"

"Yes, Steve!"

She heard him move closer, curiosity about to make her a nervous wreck. Then she felt something warm and furry and wiggly being placed in her hands, and felt a wet swipe across her chin right before her first whiff of puppy breath.

She opened her eyes and laughed as she tried to avoid the enthusiastic tongue.

"Oh, Steve, how did you know?"

The little collie was yipping with delight. Tegan petted her, trying to calm her down.

"You said one time that you never got to have a dog."

She didn't remember telling him that, but it was so like Steve to remember a small detail she'd already forgotten.

He pulled her to her feet, puppy and all, and said, "Come look."

She moved into the circle of his arms at the open door. Out in the yard, snow had begun to flutter down.

"It probably won't stick," she said sadly.

"I know, but at least we had our very first white Christmas."

After a few minutes, they closed the door.

After feeding the hungry puppy, who yawned and snuggled contentedly into her box for a nap, Tegan took Steve's hand.

Walking backward, tugging him along, she said, "Come on. I have one last present to give you."

Steve smiled.

Fourteen

Steve let her lead him back to the fireplace, and to the quilt spread in front of the hearth. He seemed just as anxious for this moment as she was.

The gifts had been wonderful, the puppy, a delight, but the waiting was over. She'd been patient...sort of...and had abided by his schedule. Now she needed to show him with her body and soul just how she felt about him.

Tegan shivered as Steve raised her hand to his lips and grazed his tongue over her knuckles with a whisper softness. He pulled her against him, wrapping his arms around her and cupping her head in his palm to hold her close to his chest.

She breathed in the male scent of him and closed her eyes to savor every sensation. The soft silk of his robe slithered underneath her fingers as she smoothed the fabric away from his chest. She smiled when she encountered his nipple, a hard little nub aching to be touched. Stroking it softly, she enjoyed Steve's twitch and sharp breath.

Tilting her chin up, he bent his head to hers, taking possession of her in a kiss that left them both breathless. She accepted the gentle invasion of his tongue, sucking it into her mouth. The groan that came from deep in his throat only added to her pleasure.

One kiss blurred and blended into another. Nothing existed but touch and taste. And each was taking as though another chance would never come.

She whimpered when he took one last, deep drink from the wine of her mouth and pulled back. She snuggled her head into his hand when he pushed her hair from her face, locking it behind her ear, and let his fingers glide down her chin.

"You know, I've always had a fantasy about making love in front of a fireplace."

She just stood, with her arms locked around his waist, her hips and thighs melded against his.

"Barns and fireplaces," she teased. "Do you ever make love in a bed?"

His husky laugh rippled over her skin. "Give me time. We'll get there."

"Then by all means, let the fantasy begin."

He was patience personified, lifting his hands to explore the contours of her face as though he were blind and memorizing her by touch. Her nightgown impeded his search so he moved his fingers to follow the line from under her ear, around the curve, to slide around the vee in tantalizing torture.

He turned her away from him by her shoulders. With infinite tenderness, he removed the band from her hair and unwound her braid, sliding his fingers through the rippled mass again and again. When Tegan doubted she could bear it any longer, he began opening the buttons of her gown, one by one, all the way to her waist with a teasing slowness. It was titillating to observe him undressing her, yet not be able to see anything of him but his hands.

He grazed the swell of her breast as he slipped her gown off her shoulders. It drifted past her hips to pool on the floor at her feet. She was panting softly by the time he slid his hands up her ribs, finally moving to cup her fullness in his long, tanned fingers.

He placed nipping kisses along the nape of her neck. He captured her earlobe and bit gently, causing her breath to catch in her throat. She sensed he was watching her as intently as she was watching his hands, and it made her pulse beat wildly.

The firelight danced on her skin. The whisper of his warm breath played on her shoulder and made her nipples harden to aching peaks.

He squeezed the roundness of her breasts into his palms and she had to bite her lip to keep from crying out. Her gasps were ragged.

Obeying his urging for her to face him again, she met his eyes and in that instant, time stopped. She memorized the look of passion on his face before letting her eyes feast on the perfection of his body.

Catching the tip of her tongue between her teeth, she smiled a delightfully wicked smile as she forced him to endure the same torture he had put her through. She slowly pushed his robe from his shoulders, letting him shrug out of it and toss the silk away.

She stroked the thick patch of dark brown hair that fanned across his chest and narrowed to a pencil-thin line before it disappeared beneath his waistband. Trailing her nails back to his shoulders, she scraped them gently down his skin as she bent her head to take the tiny bud of his nipple into her mouth. His body jerked as she licked her lips and grazed them over the little nub, flicking it with the end of her tongue.

His breathing was a hoarse rasp, hers an octave higher but just as labored. Clutching her shoulders, he pulled her away and demanded equal time. Her head fell back as he kissed and suckled at her breasts. Her eyes closed against the sensations, she stroked his head, his hair warmed by the fire.

Kicking off his pajama bottoms, he pulled her down to the quilt, moving with her in a tangle of arms and legs. He covered her with hungry kisses, traveling down her ribs, past her naval, her hips, and finally her thighs.

He covered her with his body again and this time, as he pressed her to his chest, they both groaned. Grabbing her buttocks, he pulled her fully against him. Her skin, already sensitized, responded dizzyingly to his slightest touch. And the place where their bodies were melded was a fire storm of sensation.

He pulled away to kiss her again, but Tegan stopped him, suddenly bold. Pushing him onto his back, she caressed her way from his collar to his stomach, stopping when his muscles spasmed tightly. With a smile worthy of a temptress, she used just her nails to graze the length of his arousal, and a heady sense of power came with his ragged moan. His body jerked when she took his heated length into her hand.

Tegan feasted on the sight of him. He was perfect; the image of male sexuality. He groaned again, turning his head restlessly as she learned every nuance of him. Tegan suddenly made the incredible discovery that passion could be rich and reckless. The sounds he made deep and low in his throat had her giddy with the realization that she was the one bringing him to this.

She wanted it all—to touch him, taste him, hear him, smell him, watch him. All at one time. Nothing in her life had ever seemed more right, more perfect.

She shifted to kneel beside him, exhilarating at the potent control she felt, the joy she experienced at knowing she was bringing him so much pleasure. With delicious agony, she slowly lowered her head and replaced her hand with her mouth.

His hips came off the floor as he gasped for air. She smiled against him, unable to contain the sweet laughter that bubbled up inside her. Shaking fingers buried themselves into her hair and Tegan knew he was fighting for control with every ounce of strength he possessed.

She let him move her away, pulling her beside him. He buried his face in her neck as he clutched her to him. "You have to stop," he breathed raggedly against her skin.

"Why?" she teased with pretended innocence, running her fingers through his hair and down his cheek.

"You know why. I'm about to explode. Besides, it's your turn."

Despite her confidence of a moment before, Tegan suddenly fought anxiety, a woman's terribly private fear of looking foolish. Banishing the negative thoughts, Tegan concentrated her entire being on Steve and what he was doing to her.

He quickly proved his skill to excite was more than equal to hers. Her body was on fire. Every inch of skin was alive so that she moved fitfully on the quilt.

Steve feasted on the sight of her. He could hardly contain the responses she evoked in him. She was so sensitive, his lightest touch made her moan and arch to him. He slipped his hand down to caress the sensitive inside of her leg, never quite touching the aching center of her until he knew she could stand it no longer. Then he gave her what her body craved, stroking her in an ancient, primal rhythm until her pleasure came hot and powerfully. A pure, sweet sense of male satisfaction spread through him as he watched her fly, and his own body screamed for the same release.

Positioning himself between her welcoming thighs, he waited until she urged him to come to her before uniting their bodies at last. She wrapped her arms and legs around him instinctually, and it was nearly his undoing.

When he slipped his arms underneath her so that they were as close as two humans could possibly be, he knew a wholeness, a sense of oneness such as he had never felt before. He stilled inside her and held his breath, absorbing every sensation as it came.

"Steve." His name was the sheerest gossamer, as ethereal, as delicate as the firelight that glowed around them.

Tegan reveled in the feeling of him atop her, his weight forcing her against the masked hardness of the floor. Nothing had prepared her for this. She wanted to tell him, but his mouth found hers as he began to move.

Release came again in a torrent that left her too stunned for words. She clutched him to her, absorbing his cries of pleasure as he joined her.

After claiming a moment to catch his breath, Steve lifted his weight off her, taking her with him as he rolled to lie panting on his back.

Despite the heat from the fireplace, the air soon turned their skin cool. Arms that had just moments before held her with incredible strength struggled to pull the quilt around them. But with his task complete, Steve pressed her head back to his chest and they fell asleep wrapped in each other's arms.

The cold push of a puppy's nose startled Tegan awake. The quilt had slipped down and she smiled at the four-footed friend who'd snuck out of her box. A tail wagged a plump rear end as the puppy tried to climb onto Tegan's stomach. She carefully picked the puppy up, and urged her to be quiet.

"Looks like we have a visitor," Steve said sleepily.

"She needs a name."

Steve snuggled her closer. "She looks like a giant cotton ball. How about Cotton?"

Tegan wriggled out of his grasp. "Sounds wonderful. But Cotton has to go back in her box now." She groaned as she stood. "My back is killing me."

Steve stood with her, fitting himself behind her and wrapping them both in the quilt. "Then let's get more comfortable."

"Steve, I need to put the dog up!"

After placing a kiss on her shoulder, he let her go reluctantly. "Sorry. The sight of you standing here naked distracted me."

Even though she felt guilty, Tegan carried the little one back to her box. She wanted more time with Steve and wasn't about to share. After quickly fixing a plate of warm, soft food, she put the puppy in the storeroom with a pat and a promise to be back soon.

Padding back to the living room, she stopped short when she realized Steve was gone. She found him, upstairs, stretched out on her bed.

She almost believed him asleep until his arm swept the covers back and patted the sheet beside him.

With a mock sigh, she joined him, pushing the blankets away so she could look at him while Steve pretended to snore softly. She couldn't resist lightly touching the springy curls on his chest.

She jumped when his hand caught hers. He opened one eye to look at her.

"Do you know what you're doing?"

She traced her lip with her tongue. "Absolutely."

In one fluid movement he twisted around and lay on his side, pulling her half underneath him.

"Just how much stamina do you think I have, woman?"

She smiled wickedly. "I don't know. Shall we find out?"

His answering chuckle was deep and husky, leaving no doubt as to his willingness to experiment.

Much later, Steve propped his head on his hand and watched Tegan's face as she sighed and stretched.

He dropped a kiss onto her forehead before resting back on his hand. "You are so incredibly beautiful," he whispered, running a gentle finger around her collarbone. "I love you so much."

Tegan's lashes swept down for an instant as she clenched her eyes shut. A tear slipped down her cheek but a smile curved her kiss-swollen lips.

"What are you thinking about?" Steve asked softly.

Opening her eyes, she reached up. "I didn't realize until you said them how much I've longed to hear those words. Oh, Steve, I—"

The phone rang.

Steve swore softly under his breath.

"Do you want me to get that?" he asked. "Or do you want to let the machine get it?"

She shook her head reluctantly. "You'd better get it."

Steve twisted around and grabbed the receiver from her bedside table.

"Admiral! Merry Christmas to you, too, sir."

Tegan sat up, clutching the sheet to her breasts. Suddenly, clearly, she knew what her final reservation was. She had the answer to that niggling doubt that wouldn't go away.

The Navy.

"Sir?" Steve's voice sounded confused. "Yes, sir, it will be a big change." He paused. "It was a difficult decision. And I appreciate you not rushing through those discharge papers—"

Tegan tuned out his voice as she stood. She avoided Steve's outstretched hand and left the bed. She grabbed her robe as she shut the door behind her and went downstairs.

She hadn't reached the bottom step before she heard the puppy's pitiful cries. Rescuing her, Tegan moved to sit on the couch. She petted the puppy's head absently as she stared into the fire.

How could she have been so stupid? She and Steve had talked for hours about her plans, her dreams, but they had only delved into his ideas on a superficial plane. Maybe it was because on some level she knew he didn't really want to give up that life. The admiral's call had served to jog her convenient denial about how important the Navy was to Steve.

How could their relationship survive if he had given up his dreams for her? Dear God, she'd done that once, knew how it could shrivel and destroy a soul. Oh, for now everything was fine, but what about in a year? Two years? When he became restless and bored and started hating her for making him give up his career? When would he start resenting the baby?

A voice of caution urged her to slow down, reminding her that she hadn't made Steve do anything.

But it didn't matter! She might not have asked him to do it, but she knew she'd made it clear that she'd never be involved with someone who was married to a career ever again. She'd pushed the issue, intentionally or not.

Tegan brought her knees up, snuggled the puppy close to her, and wrapped one arm around her legs.

That was why she hadn't been able to give herself fully to him, because she knew that someday he'd leave her. She wouldn't be enough to make him happy, and he'd go away.

She jumped in fright when Steve touched her shoulder. She hadn't even heard him come downstairs.

"Tegan, what's wrong?"

She looked up at him, her eyes bleak. "We've made a terrible mistake."

"What!" Steve picked up his robe and jerked it on before sitting down beside her. He took the puppy from her arms and set her free to explore the mounds of paper and boxes by the Christmas tree.

Taking Tegan's hands in his, Steve got her attention. "What was that all about?"

"Steve, I heard you. You told the admiral you were going to miss the Navy. You told him you were glad he hadn't signed your discharge papers. I heard it in your voice."

Steve looked confused at first. Then his eyebrows drew together angrily. "So that's what this is all about." He let go of her hands and sat forward with his elbows resting on his knees. "I've been wondering for weeks now why you wouldn't let go, why you wouldn't say you loved me when I saw it every day in your eyes."

Now Tegan was confused.

He rounded on her and she pulled back, surprised.

"It's not fair, Tegan. You can't make me pay for the sins of your ex-husband. I left the Navy because I was ready. It had been coming for a long time, but I didn't leave for you. I did it for me. You helped me make the decision, but you can't take the credit."

"But you said—"

"I said it was a difficult decision, and it was. I left friends and half a lifetime behind. But I didn't say I regretted it." He took her by the shoulders as though he wanted to shake some sense into her. "And if you'd listened to the whole conversation, you'd have heard me tell him that I appreciated his caution, but that I had never been more certain about anything in my life. Then I told him about the baby. And about us. Tegan, I love you. I don't know what to do to convince you. I want to spend my life with you, and I don't want to be away from you for six hours at a time, much less six months."

The dam inside her burst as he stared into her eyes. Tears streamed down her cheeks. "Oh, Steve, I want to believe you so badly."

She pressed her fingers against her lips for a moment.

"I can't bear the thought of losing you," she whispered.

Gathering her against his chest, he rested his cheek on her head. "You won't lose me, Tegan. I was lost before—then I came home to the hill country and found you. Marry me, Tegan, and make this cowboy's homecoming complete."

Tegan lifted her face to receive his kiss. With gentle fingers he wiped away her tears.

"I love you, Steve. You've brought hope and passion back into my life."

"So, is that a yes?"

Her laughter contained boundless joy. "Of course that's a yes, silly man."

His smile broadened. "Then I think a celebration is in order."

"So tell me what you have in mind."

Pressing her back to the couch, he said, "I'd rather show you."

Epilogue

"Come on, sweetheart, push!"

Tegan strained against the pain, grinding her teeth against the invectives she wanted to hurl at Steve's head.

"You push!" she growled at him.

He chuckled and placed a tender kiss against her sweaty forehead. "I would, darling, if I could."

"Come on, Mrs. Williams. One more should do it."

Tegan wanted to yank her foot out of the stirrup and kick that doctor right in the mouth.

Steve supported her as she came off the table again. Her final effort was rewarded after a moment by the sound of an indignant cry rending the air.

Lying back against the pillows, Tegan gasped for air as a slippery, wiggly little body was placed against her breast. She looked down and saw the most beautiful sight she'd ever seen. Glancing at Steve, she could only stare in wonder.

He kissed her lips so sweetly, so reverently, she thought she could die right now and her life would have been complete. Instead she stroked the tiny face that was nuzzling against her nipple and knew a moment of utter perfection.

"Welcome home, little cowboy," she whispered softly.

Steve didn't try to hide the tears in his eyes as he kissed the top of his son's head.

* * * * *

SILHOUETTE® *Desire*®

COMING NEXT MONTH

#967 A COWBOY CHRISTMAS—Ann Major

Born under the same Christmas star, December's *Man of the Month*, Leander Knight, and sexy Heddy Kinney shared the same destiny. Now the handsome cowboy had to stop her holiday wedding—to *another* man!

#968 MIRACLES AND MISTLETOE—Cait London

Rugged cowboy Jonah Fargo was a Scrooge when it came to Christmas—until Harmony Davis sauntered into his life. Could she get him under the mistletoe and make him believe in miracles?

#969 COWBOYS DON'T STAY—Anne McAllister

Code of the West
Tess Montgomery had fallen for Noah Tanner years ago, but he left her with a broken heart *and* a baby. Now that he was back, could he convince her that sometimes cowboys do stay?

#970 CHRISTMAS WEDDING—Pamela Macaluso

Just Married
Holly Bryant was expected to pose as Jesse Tyler's bride-to-be, not fall for the hardheaded man! But Jesse was a woman's dream come true, even though he swore he'd never settle down....

#971 TEXAS PRIDE—Barbara McCauley

Hearts of Stone
Jessica Stone didn't need help from anyone, especially a lone wolf like Dylan Grant. But Dylan refused to let Jessica's Texas pride—and her to-die-for looks—stand in his way!

#972 GIFT WRAPPED DAD—Sandra Steffen

Six-year-old Tommy Wilson asked Santa for a dad, so he was thrilled when Will Sutherland showed up in time for Christmas. Now if only Will could convince Tommy's mom he'd make the perfect husband for her!

MILLION DOLLAR SWEEPSTAKES (III)

No purchase necessary. To enter, follow the directions published. Method of entry may vary. For eligibility, entries must be received no later than March 31, 1996. No liability is assumed for printing errors, lost, late or misdirected entries. Odds of winning are determined by the number of eligible entries distributed and received. Prizewinners will be determined no later than June 30, 1996.

Sweepstakes open to residents of the U.S. (except Puerto Rico), Canada, Europe and Taiwan who are 18 years of age or older. All applicable laws and regulations apply. Sweepstakes offer void wherever prohibited by law. Values of all prizes are in U.S. currency. This sweepstakes is presented by Torstar Corp., its subsidiaries and affiliates, in conjunction with book, merchandise and/or product offerings. For a copy of the Official Rules send a self-addressed, stamped envelope (WA residents need not affix return postage) to: MILLION DOLLAR SWEEPSTAKES (III) Rules, P.O. Box 4573, Blair, NE 68009, USA.

EXTRA BONUS PRIZE DRAWING

No purchase necessary. The Extra Bonus Prize will be awarded in a random drawing to be conducted no later than 5/30/96 from among all entries received. To qualify, entries must be received by 3/31/96 and comply with published directions. Drawing open to residents of the U.S. (except Puerto Rico), Canada, Europe and Taiwan who are 18 years of age or older. All applicable laws and regulations apply; offer void wherever prohibited by law. Odds of winning are dependent upon number of eligible entries received. Prize is valued in U.S. currency. The offer is presented by Torstar Corp., its subsidiaries and affiliates in conjunction with book, merchandise and/or product offering. For a copy of the Official Rules governing this sweepstakes, send a self-addressed, stamped envelope (WA residents need not affix return postage) to: Extra Bonus Prize Drawing Rules, P.O. Box 4590, Blair, NE 68009, USA.

SWP-S1195

**Who needs mistletoe when
Santa's Little Helpers are around?**

Santa's
Little
Helpers

brought to you by:

Janet Dailey

Jennifer Greene

Patricia Gardner Evans

This holiday collection has three contemporary stories
celebrating the joy of love during Christmas.
Featuring a BRAND-NEW story from *New York Times*
bestselling author Janet Dailey, this special anthology
makes the perfect holiday gift for you or a loved one!

FREE GIFT
with purchase
see inside

You can receive a beautiful 18" goldtone rope
necklace—absolutely FREE—with the purchase of
Santa's Little Helpers. See inside the book for details.

Santa's Little Helpers—a holiday gift you will want
to open again and again!

Silhouette®

SLH95

Three brothers...
Three proud, strong men who live—and love—by

THE CODE OF THE WEST

Meet the Tanner brothers—Robert, Luke, and
now, Noah—in Anne McAllister's

COWBOYS DON'T STAY
(December, Desire #969)

Tess Montgomery had fallen for Noah Tanner
years ago—but he left her with a broken heart *and*
a baby. Now he was back, but could he convince
her that sometimes cowboys do stay?

Only from

SILHOUETTE®

Desire®

Hearts of Stone

Three strong-willed Texas siblings whose rock-hard
protective walls are about to come tumblin' down!

The Silhouette Desire miniseries by

BARBARA McCAULEY
concludes in December 1995 with
TEXAS PRIDE (Silhouette Desire #971)

Raised with a couple of overprotective brothers,
Jessica Stone *hated* to be told what to do. So when
her sexy new foreman started trying to run her life,
Jessica's pride said she had to put a stop to it. But
her heart said something *entirely* different....

HOS3

ANGELS AND ELVES
by Joan Elliott Pickart

Joan Elliott Pickart brings you her special brand of humor tales of the MacAllister men. For these carefree bachelors, predicting the particulars of the MacAllister babies is much easier than predicting when wedding bells will sound!

In November, Silhouette Desire's *Man of the Month,* Forrest MacAllister, is the reigning Baby Bet Champion and a confirmed "uncle." Until his very pregnant, matchmaking sister introduced him to Jillian Jones-Jenkins, he never would have thought that the next baby he bets on might be his own!

Experience all the laughter and love as a new MacAllister baby is born, and the most unpredictable MacAllister becomes a husband—and father in *Angels and Elves,* book one of THE BABY BET.

In February 1996, Silhouette Special Edition celebrates the most romantic month of the year with FRIENDS, LOVERS...AND BABIES! book two of THE BABY BET.

BABBET1

You're About to Become a

Privileged
Woman

Reap the rewards of fabulous free gifts and benefits with proofs-of-purchase from Silhouette and Harlequin books

Pages & Privileges™

It's our way of thanking you for buying our books at your favorite retail stores.

PROOF OF PURCHASE
SD-PP75
Offer expires October 31, 1996

Harlequin and Silhouette—
the most privileged readers in the world!

For more information about Harlequin and Silhouette's PAGES & PRIVILEGES program call the Pages & Privileges Benefits Desk: 1-503-794-2499

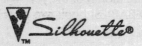

SD-PP75